I was enchanted
by the old ballroom

I imagined the gas lamps shining down on a glamorous gathering of women in evening gowns and men in black cutaways. I could almost hear the music of the orchestra striking up a waltz, and I unconsciously began moving my feet in time to the haunting rhythms.

I was smiling and humming to myself, carried away by the romance of the scene my mind played, when I suddenly noticed the look on the face of the elderly housekeeper who had accompanied me.

It was one of horror.

"What is it?" I whispered, moving towards her.

She backed away and said hoarsely, "It's *her*. She's here, in this room...."

SECRET AT ORIENT POINT

PATRICIA WERNER

Harlequin Books

TORONTO • NEW YORK • LONDON
AMSTERDAM • PARIS • SYDNEY • HAMBURG
STOCKHOLM • ATHENS • TOKYO • MILAN

Acknowledgements

Many thanks to Andrew Marlay
for consultation on costumes;
to Marlene Hamerling
for advice on Jewish names;
to Steve Hadley,
Director of the Oysterponds Historical Society;
and to Andrea Budy
for sharing thoughts about her inn.

Published April 1988
ISBN 0-373-32018-3

CHAPTER ONE

AT THE EASTERNMOST TIP of the North Fork of Long Island, the land flattens and the waters of the Long Island Sound merge with Gardiner's Bay. I had just arrived on the afternoon ferry from New London, where I had traveled by steamer and by rail from my aunt's home in Belfast, Maine.

A strange mixture of curiosity and nervousness filled me as I clung to the railing while the ferry eased into the slip, for I was taking in sights, sounds and smells from a forgotten part of my life.

Across the road stood the formidable Orient Point Inn with its several wings. The knowledge that I, too, would soon be keeping a hotel made me look sharply at this imposing structure toward which many of the ferry passengers hurried, but my reverie was interrupted by the approach of an elderly man. He was stoop shouldered, and as I was rather tall for a woman, he thrust his head forward and looked up at me questioningly. "Would you be Miss Erika Barlow?"

My smile brightened and I put out my hand. "That I am. Could you be Teddy Jordan?"

He nodded and took my hand, amazement registering in his pale eyes. "'Tis hard to believe you're the little yellow-headed thing we saw into the hands of your Aunt Isadore so many years ago. You're all grown-up now, and pretty, at that."

I laughed in embarrassment. "I'm twenty-four."

"Nearly a quarter of a century." Sadness touched his eyes briefly and he looked away. He pointed to a sturdy wagon nearby. "Maude says, 'Take the buggy. We want Miss Erika arrivin' in style.' But I says, 'No, she'll be needin' the wagon for the luggage.'"

He inquired about said luggage and then went to fetch it as I walked to where the wagon stood with its pair of dark bay mares.

Presently my steamer trunk, hatbox and two carpetbags were atop the conveyance. "All right now, Missy," said Teddy. "If you don't mind a few bumps and jars, I'll have you there in no time."

I climbed up and settled myself, and Teddy came around to the driver's side. Most of the phaetons, surreys and other horse-drawn conveyances had fought their way out of the crowded landing and were pulling up to the hitching posts in front of the inn, which we now left behind. To our left was thick vegetation, scrub pine and wetlands, and a path that led to the beach beyond. Finally we rounded a thick hedge, and I laid eyes on the hotel built by my grandfather twenty-five years ago. A flood of memories assailed me, and when Teddy tried to smile at me, there was moisture in his eyes.

"Oh, Teddy," I said, feeling the pull at my heart as well. "Do you think we can make a go of it?"

"It only wants for some life in it, and if you've made up your mind to open up the place, I see no reason you can't. The railroad's bringin' more people out this way, though most of the locals hereabouts don't like it much. But those city folks got to have some place to go summers."

The enormity of the task of running my own hotel caused me a fresh wave of doubt as I looked at the four-story building we were approaching. The brick facade with its sagging wraparound porch looked smaller than I remembered it. Of course I had been four years old when I left here to live with my aunt in Maine. My memories of the hotel were very dim, but already, as I gazed at the dormer windows of the attic, I recalled playing there—against my mother's strictest orders, of course.

I had been too young to understand the things that happened here and the reasons the hotel had been closed twenty years ago. I was twelve before I learned the truth about how my mother died.

As we pulled into the weed-filled yard in front of the hotel, I recalled the uncertainty in my aunt's eyes as she had bidden me goodbye only a few days earlier. Now I saw the same uncertainty in Teddy's veiled look. Was I right to reopen these doors that had been closed for so long?

I had no immediate family, no other prospects of fortune, and I was unmarried. But I was the owner of this property left to me in trust by my father in his will. I had told my aunt that if I were to have a future I had to try to make something of the old hotel.

Aunt Isadore had looked at me with some surprise when I told her I meant to run the place myself, and now, looking at these remote surroundings, the weather-beaten shutters on the boarded-up windows, I realized it would be a bigger job than I had thought. Still, I tried to take heart as we pulled to a stop in front of the entry portico. It was only September, and I had nine months to see to repairs. Meanwhile I would have to learn everything I could about running a hotel, and I hoped I could rely heavily on the caretakers, Maude and Teddy Jordan.

A plump, gray-haired woman with a large apron covering her brown homespun dress emerged onto the porch and made her way down the steps as Teddy helped me climb down. She bustled toward me, peering at me through wire-rimmed spectacles.

"Lord 'a mercy, can it really be our own little Erika?"

"Hello, Maude," I said as she hugged me in her ample embrace. Her cheeks, though lined, were still soft.

"Oh, Maude, it's good to see you," I said, smiling at her glistening blue eyes, her round face, her beaming smile.

"My goodness, you've grown into a tall thing," she said, standing back and eyeing my full length.

"I'm five-foot-six," I said, grinning, and I knew that with my hair piled under my straw bonnet, I must look even taller.

She clasped her hands together and shook her head. "And you seemed so little the day your aunt came for you." Her lower lip trembled slightly as she said, "I always wondered how you and your aunt would get on together with your poor mother gone, God bless her, and your father..." She swallowed, choking off the rest of her words, but I knew she was thinking about my father's being drowned when his ship had broken up on rocks in a gale in the Auckland Islands, two hundred miles south of New Zealand.

I smiled tenderly, glad of these two friends. I could see the sympathy in Maude's and Teddy's expressions as they looked at me. My aunt had told me that I resembled my mother in the face and in the coloring of my hair, which was very blond.

"Well, come in now," Maude was saying. "You'll be wanting to freshen up."

"Yes," I said, my gaze wandering along the tall, narrow windows of the downstairs. I could see how neglected the shutters were. So, too, the pillars that supported the shingled porch roof.

Once I stepped into the entrance hall, I saw that the Jordans had kept the lobby in good condition. The fine oak wainscoting and the desk against the opposite wall gleamed with polish. Even the intricately carved newel posts and the balustrades of the grand staircase shone.

"It looks the same," I heard myself say as I followed Maude through the lobby, mostly in shadow because of the boarded-up windows. She led me up the wide staircase, and on the second-floor landing she paused and turned to me with a look of hesitation.

"I wasn't sure what rooms you'd want," she said.

"My rooms?"

"We don't keep more than two or three rooms fixed up, since we only get the odd traveler now and then."

"Oh, any room will be fine," I assured her.

"I thought you might like to have a look at your mother's room," she said, fiddling with her apron.

"Oh." I don't know why the notion jarred me, and I fumbled for an appropriate response. "I...of course."

She beckoned me to follow her up another flight of stairs to the third floor. The hallway was almost completely in shadow, there being only a slit of light from a shuttered window at the end of the hall. But I came on steadily behind her until she stopped in front of a paneled door that had a fresh coat of reddish-brown paint, though the other closed doors that lined the hall were the mottled brown color of peeling paint.

Maude opened the door, and sunlight struck my eyes. I had to blink after being in the dark passages, for I was now standing in a bright room with green-and-gold-patterned wallpaper. A heavy bed with a half-tester and tufted bedspread was adorned with fringed silk bed hangings with lace side curtains. The windows were draped with the same materials as the bed hangings. There was not a speck of dust in the room.

"I keep everything the way she left it," said Maude as she bent to smooth a wrinkle out of the bed cover, and then with a shock, I realized that on the dressing table were hairbrushes, atomizers, powder boxes and a gilt hand mirror, all positioned as if someone were just about to sit down to complete her toilet.

It would be mad to think that Maude had kept the room in readiness for my mother, who had been dead for twenty years. Then I realized that she must have laid these things out for me, thinking I might like the room for myself.

I was about to speak when my eye fell on a picture in an oval frame that hung on the wall to the side of the dresser. A young woman with light-colored curls gazed romantically out of the photograph. The half smile looked familiar, and I realized it was the same expression I often wore.

Maude came to stand by me. "She was pretty, wasn't she?" I said.

"That she was." Maude shook her head. "Poor girl, it was her undoing."

I realized she was referring to my mother's death, and I wanted to ask more. My aunt had been loath to talk of it, yet when I was old enough, she finally told me how Julie Ann had been found at the bottom of a windmill with a man named Gerhard Langermann—his hands still on her throat.

The picture it conjured caused my mouth to feel dry, but it no longer held the same horror it had at first. I was left only with the burning question, why? For I knew that Gerhard Langermann had been my mother's lover.

"The picture was taken on her nineteenth birthday," said Maude.

I wanted to study the portrait at length, but now was not the time. "The room is lovely," I said. "I'd hate to disturb anything here. I mean if you have another room, I would prefer it."

I hadn't meant to embarrass her, and I was surprised that instead of being miffed at my refusal to sleep in Julie Ann's bed, she looked at me queerly and said, "No, your sleep would most likely not be disturbed elsewhere."

As I followed her out of the room and back toward the staircase, her words sank in. *My sleep would most likely not be disturbed.* Turning the words over in my mind, I decided that she simply meant that thoughts of my mother while sleeping in her room might have had a disturbing effect on me.

Maude led me to an airy suite of rooms on the second floor facing the sound. I was also afforded a view of the kitchens below to my left, the stables across the yard and the white clapboard building that had housed the servants, its paint peeling now. Beyond that was the path leading through a thicket of undergrowth to the boat house and the beach, rocky at the water's edge.

The beach stretched eastward, where dense growth hid the Orient Inn at the end of the island. To the west, the tangled thicket rose to a bluff that led steeply down to the water. I found myself anxious to explore the beach, for never had I felt so drawn to nature as here where the land reached out to the ocean, with the thin blue-green rise of land far out on the other side of the sound.

"The tip of the island is a special place," Maude said. "That's why the folks hereabouts don't like all this tourist trade everyone's talkin' about. The folks in the village like to keep it peaceful."

I turned back to her, reminded of all my new concerns as a hotel keeper. "I hope we will be able to hire a reliable staff," I said. "Do you think many people from the village will be interested in employment?"

"You'd do well to advertise in the *Suffolk Weekly*, I'd say. Lots of folks in Greenport will be lookin' for work if the fishing and shipbuilding yards there don't suit 'em."

"Yes, of course." Greenport, five miles from the village of Orient, was a thriving center and the logical place to seek help, what with its railroad terminus and dock for the ferry to Shelter Island.

Maude said, "I'll bring you some tea, unless you'd like to come down to the kitchens yourself."

"Oh, yes, I'd like that. Just give me half an hour to change and to air some of my clothes. Then I'd love a hot cup of tea. I'm famished."

"Just come down when you're ready then. You remember the way. The corridor to the left of the desk goes out toward the back. The main kitchen's just along the walk."

"Thank you, Maude." I couldn't resist smiling at her solicitousness. "I'm happy to be here."

She reached out and squeezed my hand. "We're mighty glad to have you, my dear. I hope everything works out."

I helped Teddy with my large trunk, then I unpacked the things that would need airing right away. There was a dressing table with a hinged top, and as I unpacked the contents of my small carpetbag, I found a good place to put the packet of letters I had brought with me. My mother's letters. I held the packet thoughtfully for a moment, then stuck it down in a compartment in the dresser and closed the lid.

I hurried downstairs. As I crossed the lobby, I heard a footfall, and I thought Teddy might have come in, but when I looked, there was no one there. I stood for a moment in the quiet, and yet even as my eyes grew accustomed to the shadows, I could see no one.

"Teddy?" I called. But no one replied. I shook my head, deciding the sound had been just the settling of the old building, but when I turned to go, I heard it again. There was the distinct creak of a board coming from the staircase.

I retraced my steps around the desk, and then gasped. Someone had been watching me from between the balusters. My heart hammered at the unexpected appearance of a face, and of a form crouching beneath the railing, and I stared at him for some seconds.

By the time I found my voice, he was gone. Even as I blinked, he slipped back into the shadows and disappeared. I did not linger in the shadowy lobby, but gathered my skirts and ran down the corridor that led to the back door and along the boardwalk to the kitchens. I stopped when I got to the kitchen buildings, which stood a little apart from the hotel, and gathered my breath. I turned to stare at the rows of shuttered windows along the back of the main building. Whom had I seen inside?

I stepped into the main kitchen to find Maude at the center table rolling out pie dough. "Well, and are you ready for your tea now?" She turned from her work to lift the kettle from the top of the big iron stove and pour water into a teapot. She had piled a plate with sandwiches, as well.

"Maude," I said, moving to take a seat in a spindle-back armchair next to the long wooden table on which she worked. "There was someone on the stairs when I came down. It wasn't Teddy. Is there anyone else about?"

She looked up. "A man, was it?"

"Yes," I nodded, realizing that my heart was still racing.

"That's just old Pepys."

"Pepys?"

"You mustn't mind him, Erika. He's harmless. You probably don't remember him. Your mother bade me to keep you from him when you were little." She touched her temple. "He's got something missing here, poor creature, and as long as I can remember he's had no home. We feed him and let him sleep in the stables. He does the odd job, feeds the animals. He's a strange one, but he wouldn't do you any harm."

"Why was he staring at me like that?"

"Curious, most likely. He was fond of your mother, too," she said, then pressed her lips together.

"He's really been here that long?"

"Aye. I don't rightly know when he first came here or where he came from. He was young then, but still daft." She was filling the pie with peaches, but she stopped and looked at a spot in the center of the room, as if seeing a picture in her own mind. "Sometimes he'd follow Miss Julie Ann down to the beach and along the rocks where she liked to go."

She stopped talking then. With a little tilt of her head and a frown, she resumed arranging the fruit in the pie.

I thought I knew what she had been about to speak of, and I wanted to hear more. Though I had told myself that I didn't want to dwell on the past, I couldn't resist the chance to question Maude. She was most likely keeping some things from me—things I had found out the day I'd discovered my mother's letters to Gerhard Langermann.

"Pepys used to follow her along the beach?" I asked.

Maude lifted one shoulder as if she didn't think the matter worth discussing, but I leaned forward. "Wasn't there a secluded cove? Aunt Isadore told me they used to picnic there."

She gave a little gasp. I rose to take hold of her arm.

"I'm sorry, Maude. I didn't mean to say it like that. Here, let me pour the tea."

As if uncertain what to do next, Maude sat down heavily at the table, watching me pour the tea. I placed a cup in front of her and stirred milk into my own.

Maude was glassy-eyed. "We shouldn't speak ill of the dead," she murmured.

I sipped my tea thoughtfully and then said gently, "It's all right, Maude. I don't think it's wrong for me to want to know about my mother. I remember how beautiful she was and I loved her. It's not disrespect I feel, it's just that I . . ." I gave up trying to express myself and sat back to stare at the handle of my cup.

I heard Maude rattle her spoon. When I lifted my eyes, she was gazing at me, her eyes more focused now. She took in a breath and sighed, her bosom rising and falling slowly. Then she gave me a little nod. "It's right that you should know. For if you don't know the truth about your mother, you'll only be the victim of the gossips. Thank goodness not many speak of it nowadays, at least not in my hearing."

I nodded, knowing that when my mother was murdered by her lover, Gerhard Langermann, some had said it was God's vengeance, though I wasn't sure I would put it in exactly those terms.

Maude gazed toward the window where the afternoon light had deepened the autumn colors. "Aye, Julie Ann and Gerhard Langermann loved each other since childhood, though he was five years older. She was fifteen and he twenty when they carved a heart with their initials in it in the old beech tree. Serious they were, too. Gerhard worked hard on his father's farm, aiming to build her a house when they came of age and married."

"But they didn't marry," I said.

"No. Her father, your grandfather, William Lundfeld, thought himself a religious man. I can't say he was right, though, for all his Puritan ancestry. For using religion to keep those two apart only led to tragedy, didn't it?" She sat with her lips in a firm line, silently condemning my grandfather for his mistakes.

"What happened?" I whispered.

"Your grandfather forbade the marriage because the Langermanns were Jewish. He refused to see his daughter marry a non-Protestant. Gerhard's family was equally stubborn." Maude shook her head. "They all had endless squabbles, they did—all but the two lovers.

"William was set on marrying Julie Ann to Edward Barlow, captain of one of his ships. Captain Barlow agreed to quit the sea and run the hotel William planned to build." She gestured vaguely at our surroundings. "So he built it."

I nodded, for most of this I knew. "But she still loved Gerhard, didn't shé?" I had never seen a picture of

Gerhard Langermann, but I could imagine him, for my mother had more than once made reference in her letters to his dark wavy hair—how she loved to run her fingers through it.

"I'm afraid life at sea had not given Captain Barlow those qualities a man needs to be a hotel proprietor. Uncouth he was, and his language foul, though I'm ashamed to be tellin' you all this."

I sought to reassure her. "It doesn't hurt me, honestly." I smiled. "I remember the night he picked up a man by his collar and threw him over the banister. I must have been three-and-a-half."

"Lord 'a mercy, I thought that was the end. Your grandfather was always scoldin' him, tellin' him he'd better whip himself into shape. Half the time poor Miss Julie Ann would be up in her room cryin' her heart out." Maude lowered her voice. "Can't say as I blamed her for runnin' after Mr. Gerhard for comfort. He used to wait for her down the beach, I believe, and she'd flee the cursin' and fightin' that went on in this place and go to him."

Maude's cheeks became tinged with color. "I prayed in church, prayed for all their souls, but it didn't seem to do any good. I hoped she could find love in her marriage, but she didn't, not with her husband drinkin' and insultin' the guests. 'Course I know he just wasn't suited for it. He'd been lured to shore by thoughts of big profits and a pretty bride, but his heart wasn't in it."

"So he went to sea again."

"That he did. Left the running of the hotel to your mother. Oh, he came back some. Only made short voyages up and down the coast. Until the last time."

I leaned forward, breathless as the story that had so fascinated me for years unfolded. "Did my mother still see her lover?"

"Your grandfather tried to make sure she never saw him. He and Gerhard's father agreed that the best thing would be for Gerhard to marry quickly." Maude shook her head. "God forgive me, maybe I should've told the old man the few times I knew she slipped out. But she had me wrapped around her little finger, she did, though I would've told had I known how it would end."

"Now Maude, you can't blame yourself for that."

It took her some moments to get herself under control, and then she continued to talk as if needing to unburden herself. "After a few months, Julie Ann seemed to accept her fate, poor girl. She had to when Gerhard married. But didn't I hear her cryin' herself to sleep? And she would still slip out nights to wander the beach. Sometimes I could hear her laughter echoing from the rocks that form that little cove just beyond the bluff. I knew she must be sneakin' off to see him again, though it couldn't have been often, what with him livin' on the South Fork then."

"And Gerhard's wife?"

"Lydia Schecter. Her father had land on the South Fork, and Gerhard and his new wife settled on it. I hoped your mother would stop seein' him then."

"But she didn't."

Maude gave a noncommittal shrug, but I know she wanted to tell me so that she wouldn't have to bear the guilt of keeping silent about Julie Ann's unfaithfulness. But tearing at her was the secret she thought she had kept from the four-year-old child who had been taken away from this place the day Gerhard Langermann was hanged for murdering his mistress.

"You can tell me, Maude." My eyes held hers, and I took her cold hands in mine. I needed her to confirm what I had concluded from reading between the lines of my mother's letters; from the fact that my father sent me to live with my aunt rather than raise me himself; and from the fact that I rarely heard from him until word came that he had been swept to sea and his ship broken up in the Aucklands.

"Your mother was with child, carrying you," Maude said. "She was five months gone when Captain Edward made one of his visits home—maybe only the second or third visit since they'd been married only a year before. When he saw her belly, he flew into a rage. I didn't want to hear them, so I came in here, but she ran down here to escape him, thinkin' he'd hit her and hurt her child. So I held her when she came to me, the tears streamin' down her face. He came in here and cursed her for her unfaithfulness right in front of me. Drunk he was, too."

Maude's face was crimson, and I saw her difficulty in going on, so I said it for her. "He said I was a bastard, didn't he, Maude?" I found that tears were spilling out from under my own lids even though the idea was not new to me. It was seeing Maude's emotion that undid me, making real for me the scene that must have taken place in this very kitchen.

"He said he knew who my real father was, didn't he?"

Her eyes were round with shame, and she nodded. Relief at not having to withhold the truth from me evidently mingled with the horror of having me acknowledge my own illegitimacy.

"It's all right, Maude. I found some of her old letters. I guessed. It's better to know the truth."

After a few moments, she found her voice again. "I tried to stop the rumors. But the servants had seen her sneak off with Gerhard in the early days when she was so unhappy. I suppose she couldn't help herself. What love was there for her here, with her husband showing up drunk and foulmouthed like he did?

"The captain made Miss Julie Ann hold up her head though. He even stayed home for the birth. They all thought he'd reformed, and maybe he had. At least he didn't drink so much. He kept a firm hand on his wife and tended to the hotel as best he could. Claimed you as his own at your baptism, even though he knew it wasn't so. But I could never say those two were happy. Too much damage had been done by then."

"And the lovers?"

She shook her head. "They kept away from each other after that. At least I thought so. Gerhard's wife, Lydia, gave him a son. They named him David."

The light had faded as we'd been talking, and we hadn't yet lit the kerosene lamps. Outside, the heavy brick facade of the hotel was in shadow, and the dark greens of the trees at the edge of the yard grew deeper. I leaned forward.

"Then David Langermann," I said, hearing the quaver in my voice, "is my half brother."

CHAPTER TWO

OVER THE YEARS, I'd become fascinated with the love affair that had evidently led to my birth. I never told my aunt I had found my mother's letters, tied up in a packet and hidden among her linens, but I'd read the firm hand of Gerhard Langermann as he poured out his love for my mother before she was married. He had written of her beauty, even composing poetry inspired by his feelings.

There were also later letters from my mother to Gerhard, and I didn't know if they were ever delivered, or if she had asked for them back. Perhaps the lovers had quarreled and she had decided to keep her heartfelt declarations of love to herself.

And so I had learned much about both of them. I knew of Gerhard's wife, for in his few later letters to my mother, he wrote regretfully of Lydia, wishing he could be a better husband, but acknowledging that it was at best a marriage of convenience, for his heart would remain forever in the possession of his beloved Julie Ann.

There were other letters, too, disturbing ones. In them, Gerhard seemed to be losing his mind, and I could not tell if it were really so, or if frustration with his life only made it seem so. In those letters, Gerhard spoke of how Julie Ann had possessed him, and how they must free themselves of their obsession if they were ever to find happiness.

Now while I ate the sandwiches she had prepared, Maude rose and lit a lamp, the light flickering about the room. She did the cooking for herself and Teddy here, but the kitchen was of the proportions that a chef and staff would be able to prepare meals for a hundred. Another door led into a large pantry, where goods were kept in barrels, in sacks and in numerous ceramic and glass jars on shelves lining the walls. For the fall and winter we would be feeding only ourselves and a limited staff, but I was reminded of the endless staples we would need when the next tourist season approached.

"You say Pepys feeds the animals?" I asked Maude.

"Yes, he does." We had come out to stand on the boardwalk that led back to the hotel proper. "You can trust him with them. I suppose he understands them in his own way."

I nodded. "He can remain as stable boy then. But we'll hire a proper groom for the horses we'll need to purchase for the use of the guests."

Carrying the lamp, she led the way back to the hotel. "It's not so dark you can't see yet," she said when we got inside. "I'll just show you a bit of the rooms."

As I followed her across the creaking floorboards toward the dining room, memories began to click into place in my mind.

I don't know how the years had slipped by so fast since I had left here. I'd gone to school, kept house for my aunt, read a great deal and hiked about the countryside. I had finally realized that no one was going to offer to show me the world. The great explorers and adventurers I fantasized I would one day meet never came to Belfast, and so I realized I would have to find a way to experience the world myself.

Now, following Maude through the lounge to the west of the lobby and on into the dining room, my romantic notions seemed to create in my mind's eye the glamour I longed to see here. The round tables, bare now, would be covered with snowy-white linens, the cane chairs dusted and polished till they shone. But undoubtedly the finest features of our dining room were the six-lamp, gilt-bronze gasoliers suspended from the ceiling. Dull now, their metallic surfaces would be polished and the etched-glass shades cleaned. How beautifully the gaslight would illuminate this room, together with the wall sconces for the candles.

"There's seats enough for fifty-two, plus the tables in the lounge," she said.

"My goodness," I replied. "It doesn't seem a large number, but I can imagine how much work it'll be to feed three times that many who'll eat here in one night."

When I closed my eyes I could imagine the dining room full to capacity with waiters in white starched jackets rushing here and there. A din of laughter and conversation would fill the room. I opened my eyes again to corners now cloaked in darkness, the windows nailed shut.

"We must air out this room tomorrow," I said. "I'll ask Teddy to open up all the windows." Such a gay room. It had once glittered, full of the rustle of silk and the tread of shoes moving from the carpet that ran the length of the room to the planking beneath the tables.

"There's just the double parlor on the east side of the lobby," Maude said. "Teddy and I still keep the cottage over past the stables."

"How is the heating?" I asked.

"All the rooms have cast-iron stoves, and the suites like yours have the fireplaces, but you don't need them until October."

"It would be nice to install steam heat, but that would be a rather expensive undertaking," I said, thinking aloud. "What about the plumbing?"

"There's just the bathrooms at the end of each floor, but the water runs hot and cold. Would you be wanting to see the upstairs rooms now or do you need your rest?" she asked.

"I'm not tired." Indeed I was too excited to sleep yet, though it was too dark now to see the rooms very clearly.

She led me up the stairs to the second floor, where a sitting room looked over the back of the hotel. I passed between the shrouded furniture, the lamp illuminating the flocked wallpaper, showing moisture stains in places. Then I remembered what I especially wanted to see.

"Can we see the ballroom? I used to love it there, especially when there were dances."

I was chattering with anticipation before I noticed that Maude was frowning and looking doubtful. But at last she nodded, and I picked up a lamp to light our way to the top floor. We paused at the double doors that led to the ballroom, and Maude searched through her large jumble of keys for the right one. While she was fitting the large brass key into the lock, I eyed the ivory paint that had peeled from the gilt-edged panels of the graceful doors.

Then she threw the doors open and I felt a breeze float through the room. It startled me, and as we stepped in, Maude crossed the smooth floor to the French doors that led to the balcony on the opposite side. One of the doors was open, the old brocade drapes moving in the breeze.

She pulled the door to the balcony firmly and turned the handle to latch it shut. I was so enchanted with the ballroom that I failed to notice Maude's agitation at first. I imagined the gas lamps illuminating the room from their sockets mounted at intervals all along the walls, the gasoliers shining down on a glamorous gathering of women in evening gowns and men in black cutaways. I could almost hear the music of the orchestra playing on the stage at the end of the room and unconsciously began moving my feet in small steps to imaginary music.

I was smiling and humming to myself, carried away by the romance of the scene, when I turned and started to speak to Maude. But I drew up short, for she was looking at me with such an expression of horror that my heart seemed to rise into my throat. I looked over my shoulder to see what had disturbed her so. There was nothing behind me but the darkness and shadow of the empty stage.

"What is it?" I whispered and moved toward her.

She raised her hands in a feeble gesture, and from her paleness, I thought she might faint. Then instinctively I knew she was thinking of my mother, and her next words proved me right.

"She and Mr. Gerhard . . ." But Maude couldn't finish. I knew that watching me take small dance steps and gliding around the room had reminded her of my mother dancing, partnered by her lover. It was curious that Maude would remember them dancing together in public, but at that moment I only wanted to reassure Maude that it was me with her and not some specter of the past.

"Maude," I said, holding the light near my face, "come now, I've seen enough. The rest can wait till morning."

I led her to the doors, and she went willingly. The tune I had been humming still went round and round in my head. It was a waltz, for I enjoyed the moving, three-beated rhythm that could send couples dizzily swaying across a room.

I fancied the orchestra played the tune even now as I left the ballroom behind me and held the light for us to see our way down the staircase. Maude glanced at me queerly, and I hoped she didn't disapprove of my romantic notions. I reminded myself that it might be easy for Maude to become upset, for she had to grow used to the fact that in some of my gestures and expressions, I resembled my mother.

Seeing that Maude had regained her composure, I felt satisfied in leaving her. "Thank you for everything, Maude. I just know we'll make a go of the place. I shall rely heavily on you and Teddy."

"Of course, my dear. I'm not as young as I used to be, but it'll put some life back into me bones to be carrying out your orders. You'll tell me if there's anything you need?"

"Yes, I will."

"You get your sleep, then. Everything will seem bright and cheery in the morning. You'll see."

I had the feeling she was speaking as much to herself as to me. "Good night" I said.

"Land sakes," she said, hurrying back to me. "I forgot to get you any supper."

I laughed. "The tea and sandwiches were enough. I'm not hungry, really."

"Well, if you're sure," she finally said and bade me good night again.

I turned into my rooms and got ready for bed, then I drew up a chair next to the open window and gazed out at the stars winking over the darkness of the sound. A cloud moved across the moon, illuminating the beach, and I saw part of a ship's hull embedded in the sand, reminding me of how frequent such wrecks were.

It made me think sadly of Edward Barlow, a man I never really knew, for his ship had gone down fifteen years ago, when I was nine. The *Golden Moon* had last been seen when it left the port of Sydney, Australia, on the other side of the world. Evidently, wanting to put my mother's murder as far behind him as possible, he had shipped onto one voyage after another, ships hauling freight between continents, and had worked his way halfway around the world only to sail away on a trim little schooner that broke up on the rocks of some strange islands I had never before heard of.

There had been the occasional letter in the first years after he left, and sometimes even a little money. And of course my aunt told me that he'd left me property in trust for when I turned twenty-four, should anything happen to him. Now that I knew the bitterness he must have felt about my birth I could forgive him for not coming to see me.

I closed the window and climbed into bed. Though Edward Barlow had been crude and unsophisticated, perhaps he had hoped that my mother would learn to love him, and had drowned his disappointment in drink when she did not.

I lay with my head on my pillow, gazing at the darkness. It was a strange situation I had chosen, and yet I would be financially better off if I could manage to make the hotel bring in a good income. If in the end I found it did not suit me, I could always sell it, but it would be worth more as a working enterprise than as the moldering place it had become. It stood here now, only a symbol of ruined lives and failure. I wanted a chance to reverse that fortune.

Before I drifted off to sleep, a silhouette of the man I imagined to be David Langermann, my half brother, formed in my mind's eye. I was intensely curious about him and I knew even as I fell asleep that I would find a way to meet him.

DURING THE FOLLOWING WEEK, I hired a girl named Letty from the village to help us with the cleaning, for I wanted to make the downstairs livable even before the repairs were done. Together with Letty, Maude and I swept and scrubbed and polished. Even the old upholstery began to look decent after we'd beaten the dust out.

Teddy and Pepys worked in the yards, though Pepys remained silent whenever I was near. Sometimes when I crossed the yard to the stables or the servants' quarters or took the outside stairs to the second floor above the kitchens, I would feel someone watching me. I would pause and look about, certain it was the poor demented Pepys, but I seldom saw him. Sometimes it was just his shadow disappearing around a corner. I knew if I were patient, he would learn that he had nothing to fear from me.

Late one Wednesday afternoon, Maude came to find me in the yard, saying there was a man here to see me. She gave me his card. Johannes Berglund, Carpenter, it read.

"Where does he come from?"

She shook her head. "Says he's done work for many of the families in the village though his own home's in Southold. Says he heard someone was thinking of refurbishing the hotel, and so he came to see about applying for the job."

I raised my eyebrows. "That's enterprising of him. Tell him to wait in the parlor. I'll be with him directly."

I smoothed back my hair. I supposed the white blouse and brown muslin skirt I wore were presentable enough. One didn't dress up to do the kind of work I was engaged in now.

I entered the parlor to find a tall, ruddy-complexioned man with thick blond hair and side whiskers. He wore a high-button sack coat and held his bowler hat in his hands. His shoulders and arms seemed very muscular under the light brown serge, evidently from the work he did. He fixed his gaze on me as soon as I entered the room.

"I'm Erika Barlow," I said. "Are you Johannes Berglund?"

"I am," he replied. "And at your service." He bowed, and I smiled at his Scandinavian accent.

"Please sit down," I said, moving to take a seat on a sofa. He sat in a chair opposite me. His expression was one of confidence.

"What sort of work do you do, Mr. Berglund?"

"Any kind of woodworking. I have in my employ a number of craftsmen and artisans skilled at plastering, carpentry, even skilled in restoring fine veneers."

I gazed at him ironically. "Mr. Berglund, I don't know where you have come from, but you must have special powers of intuition to know that is exactly what I am looking for."

His blue eyes lit with humor. "I wish I could say I had the power to read minds, but I'm afraid I heard in the village that you were thinking of reopening the hotel. I thought services such as mine might be required."

A smile tugged at my lips as I nodded. "I would have to have references of course, but suppose I show you the hotel. Then if I approve of your estimate, we will discuss how the job might proceed."

"A fair proposition indeed."

He rose and I stood also, and my glance was again drawn to his eyes and the tiny lines at the corners. Character lines, my aunt would have called them.

We made a complete tour of the hotel, and I found I could converse with Johannes Berglund quite freely. I told him that while work was needed on the outbuildings, it was the hotel itself I was most concerned about at the moment. Foremost in my mind was the amount of money I would have to spend on the undertaking. We finished our survey, and he promised to call on me in two days' time with his estimates, as well as the references I had asked for.

"Miss Barlow," he said when we were standing on the porch and he was about to take his leave, "I feel certain I can give you a fair price. And as to the work—" he gave a self-assured shrug "—you will find no better."

He held my gaze for a moment, and a sense of energy about him made itself felt. Then with a nod of his lionlike head, he bade me good-day.

That evening I sat at the writing desk in my sitting room going over the old ledgers and accounts of the hotel from its former days. My father had left a bit of capital, which the attorneys who managed the trust had carefully invested for me, so that I had some funds to work with. But I became more and more convinced that the interest I had earned would not pay for everything. I groaned when I went over the inventory of what we needed, especially when I thought of new draperies and wall coverings for the halls and the ballroom. And the painters, plasterers and craftsmen would all have to be paid. Even the mirrors needed resilvering. I couldn't risk spending all my capital in case the hotel was slow in paying its own way.

It struck me that it would be advantageous to have a partner. Someone who could afford to invest some capital in my venture, but who could wait for a return on his investments for the few seasons it might take to capture a brisk trade. I did not know anyone with money, but an idea had formed. I suppose it had been there since the evening Maude and I had sat in the kitchen and she had revealed my mother's story.

Of course we never spoke of David Langermann as my half brother, at least not where anyone else could hear. To the rest of the world, Edward Barlow had claimed me as his own. But it seemed to me from what Maude said that David Langermann had done well in life. In addition to managing his lands on the South Fork, inherited from his mother, he had diversified into business. In fact Maude had heard he owned a lace mill in the town of Patchogue. If he was successful in business, might not the idea of investing in a resort hotel appeal to him?

I didn't tell Maude, for she would surely think it too bold an idea. She might even think it perverse of me that I wanted to meet him, but I couldn't help my curiosity. Of course, David Langermann might not want to see me. If he didn't know about me, he might not be pleased to have his bastard half sister land on his door-step and ask for money.

But, I told myself as I paced my sitting room in front of my writing desk, eyeing the papers I had piled up there, I was not asking for charity. I was going to offer him a business opportunity. And I needn't tell him I knew we were related. If he had been told about my mother and Captain Barlow, he would simply assume I was Edward's daughter.

Perhaps I had spent too many years making up stories, but now I had to see this other child of the only man my mother ever loved. Somehow, I felt David Langermann was part of me.

I decided the best way to proceed would be to write him a letter. By his reply I could perhaps judge what he knew of my mother and myself and perhaps get some kind of feeling for the sort of man he was.

I sat down at once and composed it. As I dipped my pen in the ink and my hand flew over the paper, I experienced a new excitement. Perhaps I knew I was treading on dangerous waters, that it had been tempting fate to come here at all and to set my hopes against all the evil that had gone on before. And now I was determined to push events as far as they would go until I had uncovered all the musty corners and thrown as much light as I could on all the secrets of my past.

CHAPTER THREE

IT WAS SOME TIME after I had posted the letter and finally told Maude what I had done, that I began to have doubts. We were in my sitting room after supper. At first she did not look up from her sewing, but then she heaved a sigh, looked over her spectacles and shook her head.

"I know you'll tell me I should have left well enough alone," I said, "but you can't blame me for being curious about my own half brother, can you, Maude?"

She leaned back in her chair, her cap askew and an exasperated expression on her face. "I don't see what good'll come of it. He'll not acknowledge you as a relative. And he'll have no reason to get involved in your plans."

No reason except perhaps an equal amount of curiosity about me, I thought. Perhaps that was what I was counting on. Of course there was the other possibility.

"He might not even know who I am," I said. "Wouldn't his father have kept such a thing from him?"

Maude shrugged. "If he knew what's best he would've. Still, young 'uns have ways of finding out about their parents. Look at you, now."

"It's been about three weeks, though, since I sent him my letter, and he hasn't replied. Even if he doesn't know me, you'd think a polite reply would be in order." Indeed, the fact that he had not replied said more to me of the fact that perhaps he did realize who I was and did not want to see me.

"He's probably a busy man, what with his lace-manufacturing company and all," Maude said, as she finished mending one of Teddy's shirts and picked up another.

"Perhaps." Still I chafed under the tension, for I had never been very good at waiting. Many times in the days since I had sent him my letter, I had had the urge to simply harness the buggy and set out to call on David Langermann himself. But although a businesswoman of my age had more freedom to come and go than one might have had in my mother's day, I could not be so brash as to call on a single gentleman without introduction or invitation.

"Maude," I said, realizing that I had never asked about his marital status, "does David Langermann have a family?"

She frowned as she jabbed a needle into the cotton shirt. "That he don't."

"One would think a man of his position, who has so much land and an income from his business, would want a family."

She finally put down her mending in her lap, seeing that my questions would persist. "Wanting a family might be one thing," she said, "but moving about freely in society would be another when your father was hanged for murder."

Of course! His mother might have kept from him the details of his father's love affair, but no one could keep from him the fact that his father was tried and hanged.

In a strange way it made me feel closer to him. David Langermann must have grown up an outcast, and having experienced my share of loneliness, I could sympathize with that. But he had not answered my letter, and it had been more than three weeks. My momentary hope slipped back into the lull I'd felt the past week or so. David Langermann could hardly be insatiably curious if he was waiting this long to respond.

I yawned and stretched. "I feel more tired than usual tonight," I said, rising and massaging the muscles in my shoulder.

"You're not used to such hard labor," Maude said. "You oughtn't be scrubbing the floors. You ought to be setting up that office of yours where you'll be ordering supplies and paying the bills when they come in."

"I don't mind scrubbing floors. And I can't afford to hire any more help just now, though I think we'll need to hire a cook to feed the builders their noonday meal. You and Letty have a lot of work, and I want to help as much as I can, at least through the winter."

"Just don't tire yourself unnecessarily." She replaced her sewing in the basket and stood, scrutinizing me. "You don't want to ruin your looks. You're a young woman, you know."

"Maude, twenty-four is not young. I have to be quite mature to run a business." She grunted and I felt myself blush, giving the lie to my assertion. Mature women did not blush, I was sure.

In the weeks that had passed I had not given any attention to my looks, dressing in plain skirts and blouses and winding my long hair into a knot secured to my head with pins. My hands were rough, my nails broken and uneven.

I walked to the bedroom to apply some lotion to my hands. I unpinned my hair, and taking my hairbrush, I brushed it thoroughly. Maude was right. I would have to maintain my appearance once we had guests. It struck me also that I needed to do something about my appearance before I met David Langermann, for I would need to make a good impression if I were to try to gain his confidence in my business venture.

Undressing and putting on my cambric nightdress and flannel dressing gown, I braided my hair, then returned to my writing desk. The fire in the fireplace was dying, but with one kerosene lamp there was enough light to write by. I composed a short note to David Langermann, inquiring if he had received my previous letter. I said I would like to call and introduce myself, for I had a business proposition I wished to discuss with him.

I was sealing the letter when I heard the soft tinkling of music. I thought it must have come from outside, but when I looked, my windows were closed. I went to the window and unlatched it, opening it to the crisp September air.

I stared out at the empty darkness and the waters of the sound. I might have told myself it was my imagination, just as I had imagined music playing the night Maude took me to the ballroom. But no, there it was again, coming faintly from somewhere above me. Lilting music that in a normal setting would have brought a smile to my face. But the ringing notes carried on the night air made the hairs on the back of my neck stand on end. There was nothing where it came from but a dark, empty ballroom.

I crossed the sitting room to my door, my heart pounding. There simply could not be any real music. Something was making me think I heard it. I paused with my ear to the door, but the sound was gone now, only an echo in my mind. Breathing hard, I slumped against the door. I reprimanded myself for becoming so frightened, checked to make sure my door was locked and returned to the bedroom.

After closing the window I climbed into bed. The weight of the covers seemed to make me feel more secure, and after I lay there for some time, my tension ebbed, and I closed my eyes. I slept badly, though, finally coming alert when the sky lightened. It was a gray dawn, and I drew the covers around me and turned over. I had no wish to rise so early.

When Letty tapped at my door some hours later, I answered groggily, "Come in."

Then I remembered the door was locked, so I threw off the covers and padded to the door, throwing it open to the surprised Letty, who was used to seeing me up and dressed by this time.

"I'm sorry if I disturbed you, Miss, but Mrs. Jordan sent me to see if you'd be down to breakfast."

"Yes, tell her I've overslept. I'll be down in a quarter of an hour." I was usually there by now, drinking a cup of coffee after my morning walk to the beach.

I pulled on stockings, drawers, camisole and petticoats hastily, followed by a day dress of cotton twill. I twisted my hair up behind my head and ran downstairs and out to the kitchen. As I took a chair, Maude eyed me from where she was lifting the coffee kettle from the cookstove. She poured my coffee and served me eggs and thick slices of bacon.

"From the looks of those circles under your eyes," she grumbled, "it don't look like you slept well." She poured herself a cup of coffee and then sat down opposite me.

"I didn't sleep very well, Maude. I thought I heard something... Did you hear anything last night that sounded like music?"

She dropped her cup in its saucer, the hot liquid scalding her hand, but she only dabbed at it with her apron. Her hands shook as she looked at me.

"What is it?" I asked.

"It's her," she breathed, smoothing her apron and looking about as if to see if anyone else were listening.

"Her?" I asked, afraid I knew what she was going to say.

She nodded. "Julie Ann."

Words stuck in my throat. I wanted to laugh, but I knew Maude was deadly serious. What was worse was that I half believed her.

I cleared my throat. "I don't understand. What I heard was like the tinkling of bells, only it was a waltz. I didn't see anything."

She shook her head. "It doesn't matter. The music goes with her. I hated to tell you. I thought you should find out for yourself." She gave a little shake of her head. "I wasn't sure she'd bother you, but of course she would. You're her own flesh and blood, and you're the one who can help her."

"Help her?"

Maude leaned toward me, speaking in a low voice. "She wants something. That's why she hasn't gone on like a spirit should."

I could only sit in stunned silence. At last I stammered, "Are... are you sure?"

She leaned back. "The night I showed you the ball-room, she was there, too. I thought you must have felt her the way you were humming that music—it's what she always wanted the orchestra to play."

My eyes widened. "Why, I just hummed the first thing that came into my head."

She nodded. "She put it there."

"You can't be serious."

Maude shook her head. "I didn't want to believe it either, at first. But don't forget, she died a violent death. She could hardly have made her peace before she went. She wants something done, that's what. You'll have to listen to her. She being your mother, you'll be able to. It's fate you're bein' here. You've come to carry out her wishes, to do whatever it is she can't do for herself."

"Maude, how can you be so sure of this? What I heard last night was fleeting. Hardly what I'd call a message from beyond."

"Haven't I been here twenty years?" she said. "There's been time to feel her presence. She started playin' her music when she knew you were comin' these past weeks. I heard it myself. She's been waitin' for you to get here."

I swallowed, not knowing what to believe. Certainly what she said about my mother's sudden and violent death was true. But I was determined to approach this as rationally as possible.

My face must have drained of color, for Maude got up to make more coffee, perhaps to revitalize me. She was mumbling and shaking her head, but I hardly noticed her, for I was too wrapped up in my own thoughts.

That afternoon I took the buggy and set out for the village, three miles away. Leaves on the trees by the road had turned deep red and gold and were dropping to the ground. Nearing the village, I passed a couple holding hands, and I smiled nostalgically as their laughter reached my ears.

I came to the old sycamore tree that marked the entrance to the village lane, and turned south, the team clopping along the lane to the post office. The village of Orient had an exceedingly quiet feeling about it as if the small community had had no part in the progress of the past century.

"Good morning, Miss Barlow." Mr. Tucker from the general store had come out on his porch and hurried down the steps to greet me.

He'd been most solicitous to me when I'd first come to the village two weeks ago with Maude. He was a jolly man with bushy mustache and gray side-whiskers. He seemed interested in seeing my hotel succeed and was one of the more friendly townspeople. Not that I had met many of them yet, but the ones I had met gave me the feeling they were reserving judgment—as if they did not readily welcome a stranger into their midst. But it was not so with Mr. Tucker or his daughter, Amelia.

"Well now," he said, after he had escorted me off the road. "What is it brings you to town? I hope you're in need of some barrels of flour or some fresh hams."

I laughed. "Mr. Tucker, you make it sound as if I am serving a hundred people already. At the moment there are only four of us. I've engaged Johannes Berglund to begin carpentry work on the hotel, but he and his workmen will go home for supper, so my new cook will only feed them at midday. I'm afraid our larders are well stocked from our last visit to your store."

"A pity. Are you sure I can't tempt you with a gallon or two of fresh apple cider?"

"Now that does sound delicious. I'll stop in as soon as I've posted my letter."

Of course I should have realized that he could read the address on the envelope I held in my hand. As he glanced at it, his bushy eyebrows shot up. I flattened the letter to my breast. Unable to think of anything else to say, I turned toward the post office and told him, "I'll just be a moment."

I stepped inside the small building and the postmistress came forward. "Good morning, Miss Barlow," she said. She was not nearly so gregarious as her neighbor the storekeeper, and she barely met my eyes as she bent over the letter and charged me for the postage. But as she looked up at me I could see disapproval in her glance.

Embarrassment began to fill me. In a village this small, everyone knew everyone else's business. No telling who the postmistress had told about my last letter to David Langermann, and here I was writing him again. I had sent my first letter with Teddy, and had not given it a second thought, but now I realized that the old-timers would know who David's father was.

She handed me my change. "Next mail doesn't leave until tomorrow, eleven in the morning."

"That will be fine," I said. Then to sound conversational, I added, "By then I may have another letter to post to my aunt in Maine. I'll send it in with Teddy in the morning if it's ready."

I bade her good-day and hurried out and down the boardwalk to the general store. The bell above the door tinkled as I entered. A high laugh came from the back room, followed by Mr. Tucker's exasperated voice, and I knew he was talking to his daughter, Amelia, a bright, pretty girl of nineteen. They both emerged, and Amelia came around the counter holding out her hands to clasp mine. When I met her on my first trip to town, we had taken an instant liking to each other. In many ways she reminded me of myself at that age, curious and romantic, a girl with a great zest for life and anxious to spread her wings.

"Erika," she said, kissing my cheek. "How wonderful to see you again. Will you stay for lunch? I'm making Papa a thick chowder and there's fresh bread."

"Well, I can hardly refuse such an invitation."

"Good. Then come round to the cottage when you've finished here." She picked up her skirts and hurried out the back of the store to the cottage behind, her brown curls bouncing on her shoulders. Mr. Tucker watched her go, his affection tinged with exasperation.

"She's a lovely girl, Mr. Tucker. You must be proud of her," I said.

"Aye. But it's not easy since her mother passed on."

"I understand." I thought I knew something of what might be occurring in the Tucker household. Amelia was a pretty young woman, high-spirited and evidently not ready to settle down. A girl like her must have had offers of marriage, which I'd no doubt she'd refused. Why?

Possibly, because like me she wanted to see what else life had to offer. Her situation was enough like my own, when I had lived with my aunt in Belfast, that I understood. I sympathized with Mr. Tucker, though. He obviously loved his daughter, but he could not provide her with the kind of excitement she longed for. As I considered the situation, I thought I might have a possible solution that would fit in very well with my own plans.

"Mr. Tucker, I don't mean to be presumptuous, but I've been thinking that I need to hire a secretary. I could only afford the help two days a week now, but in the spring and during the hotel season, I will surely need someone with writing and accounting skills such as your daughter must have used to help you. Do you think she would be interested in working for me? If you could spare her, of course.''

"Why, Miss Barlow, how generous of you. If you're sure you want her." He drew his brows together and tilted his head to one side in a gesture of fatherly concern. "I don't mind telling you I've been worried about her.''

"Well, if she's willing, I'm sure we'll get along famously," I said.

He nodded his agreement. "You go back and tell her. I'll just finish putting some things away here. I'll put your cider in the buggy when you're ready to leave.''

I paid him for the cider, then went round to the cottage where Amelia was just ladling soup out of a huge pot.

"It smells delicious," I said as I stepped into the cottage kitchen, unbuttoned my jacket and took off my hat, placing it on a bench near the door.

"Oh, please sit down and help yourself to some bread." It was still warm from the oven, and the smell of it made my mouth water.

"I'm starved," I said, and after she'd served us both, I ate with relish. I brought up my proposal that she come to work for me.

"Oh, I'm sure I could do it! I do my father's accounts, you know, and I've a passable hand. And if truth be known, I've been looking for an opportunity to do something different." She sighed, her blue eyes darting around the small cottage. "I don't mean to sound ungrateful. Papa would do anything in the world for me, but I think it's natural for a girl my age to want a bit of adventure, don't you?''

"I would hardly call being secretary to a hotel proprietress adventuresome. It'll mostly be dull paperwork. Until we open, that is. Then I'll need you to assist at the desk and as hostess in the dining room when it's very busy.''

"Oh, yes, and when the guests come, it'll be exciting. There'll be balls, won't there? And wealthy gentlemen from the city?''

"I don't know how wealthy. My hotel will cater more to the middle class. The wealthy have their own summer homes, you know.''

"Oh. But there'll be interesting people, anyway!''

Amelia's enthusiasm had got the better of me, and so I said, "Would you be willing to accompany me on a short journey in a week or so?''

"A journey!'' Her eyes lit up. "Where?''

"Only to East Hampton. We'll take my buggy and cross on the ferry. I'm not exactly sure what day we'll go.''

Amelia's father joined us then, and she hopped up to serve him some lunch. She chattered on about being employed by me, and her father beamed at us. I felt that the arrangement was going to work out satisfactorily.

"Erika says I'll even be her traveling companion.'' As she rambled on I saw her father's look change from benign pleasure to doubt and then to suspicion. The eyes that had been so merry darkened perceptibly and were watching me. I remembered that he had seen my letter, and he must know where I was planning to go.

Mr. Tucker might have known Gerhard Langermann, and I cursed myself for being so careless. My affairs were no one's business but my own, and here I had allowed gossip to start already.

I lowered my gaze, helpless to do or say anything. At a lull in his daughter's conversation, Mr. Tucker said,

"Amelia, will you return to the store and mind the customers? I will be along shortly."

"But—"

"Do as I say."

I could tell from the surprised pout on Amelia's face that such orders were rare, that her father must have something very serious on his mind to speak so. When she hurried out of the cottage, I turned to face Mr. Tucker.

"And where on the South Fork will you be taking my daughter?" he asked.

"I am going to call on David Langermann. He is considering a business proposal I have made him." I stretched the truth a little, trying to make it more acceptable for him. "I know you must find it strange that I am carrying on business with a man whose father was..." I could hear the strain in my voice, for it was difficult at best to speak of my family's intimate history to one I barely knew. But I felt Mr. Tucker had a right to know since his daughter would be working for me.

He said, "Forgive me for prying, Miss Barlow, but you must agree that the situation is highly irregular. Surely you are aware of the, er, relationship between this man's father and your late mother."

I could feel my face grow warm in spite of my resolution to appear objective. "Believe me, Mr. Tucker, I understand your concern, but to be honest with you, I need money to help finance my hotel, and Mr. Langermann has assets. I thought he might be able to invest in my project." I hoped what I said sounded plausible enough. "I am sure your daughter will be safe enough with me, but if you prefer she not accompany me to East Hampton, then I shall not take her." I lifted my head slightly. "Indeed, if you have any objections to her working for me because of the job or my family's reputation, please tell me now."

"I am not an unreasonable man, Miss Barlow. I'm just not sure I like the idea of my daughter calling on the son of a murderer, or even a single young woman like yourself doing so."

"You seem to imply, Mr. Tucker," I said, bristling in spite of my determination to remain calm, "that the son is guilty of the father's crime. Surely he has not inherited his father's verdict." I glanced away. "Or his madness."

How quickly I came to the defense of David Langermann. In that moment I believe I grew a little closer to the half brother I had yet to meet.

"You have a point, my dear, and I do not mean to condemn the man." He offered me tea from a pot Amelia had made, and we both waited until our tempers had cooled.

"Surely, Miss Barlow, you must know that gossip does not die with those who pass on. It may be wrong, and I don't believe any of the people of Orient want to hurt you, but you have a reputation to consider, and I have my daughter to think of."

I lifted my shoulders and sighed. "It seems the old hotel still has its ghosts, and it is only my wish to exorcise them."

He answered sympathetically. "Aye. That it may. And I wish you luck with it." Then he said a bit sheepishly, "I'm proud to have my daughter in your employ, Miss Barlow, so I hope you won't be withdrawing your offer. However, if part of the job requires exposing her to men with questionable reputations, then I'm afraid I'll have to decline the position on her behalf."

His expression was so full of disappointment that my heart went out to him. "Mr. Tucker, I want Amelia to work for me, too, but I won't make her go to East Hampton with me. I can take Maude or my maid, Letty, there. I really wouldn't have Amelia do anything against your wishes."

Relief showed in his eyes, and he rose and offered his hand. "Then I'll send her to you when you want her. I believe we understand each other."

"I believe we do." I shook his hand solemnly. "Amelia can come on Thursdays and stay overnight with me if that meets your approval. Then she can work Friday and return home in time to get your supper that evening."

We agreed on wages as he saw me to my carriage, and then he bustled back into the store. Amelia followed him out again as he placed two jugs of cider on the floor by my feet. Her eyes sparkled.

"Oh, Erika, I can't wait. I'll be there early Thursday, and you'll teach me everything."

"I'll look forward to it." I wondered if her father had told her the one stipulation under which she would have to work. I couldn't imagine her being pleased that she would not be accompanying me to East Hampton. But I didn't want to dampen her spirits now.

"Thank you for lunch, Amelia."

"A pleasure, Miss Barlow." She dropped me a curtsy with mock seriousness, and I laughed. In spite of her father's restrictions, I thought we would have a gay time together. I could talk to her, although she was five years my junior. She was quick and had a joie de vivre I found refreshing.

I smiled and waved as I turned my horses, hoping at the last moment that I hadn't done the wrong thing.

Perhaps my hotel was not the right place for a girl as young as Amelia, for such a business required a steady person with a firm grip on life, as I had—or at least thought I had.

Events were moving ahead, but with every step I took, I was heading for an abyss of my own creation. Of the occurrences in which I was about to become entangled, I had only myself to blame, and if I saw any of the warning signs, I failed to heed them.

CHAPTER FOUR

I PULLED into the stable yard, got down and lugged one of the cider jugs to the kitchen. I found Maude cooling a pot of beans, and when I heaved the cider onto the table, she wiped her hands on her apron.

"Good heavens, girl, Letty or Teddy should be doing that."

"Maude, I probably have twice Letty's strength, and Teddy shouldn't be doing all the heavy work."

"It just isn't right, you doin' so much around here."

"A person who owns a hotel that's been closed for twenty years has a lot of work to do. Not that you and Teddy haven't done your share, of course."

"Bah. I've no pretensions of keeping up this place by myself. It was all we could do to keep our own cottage and this kitchen, and mind the animals."

"Now Maude, don't be apologizing. And if it's any consolation I've hired a secretary. Amelia Tucker will be working Thursdays and Fridays for now, and full-time during the summer season."

"A secretary. Well, I suppose that's something. But she'll not be freeing you up from the hard work, will she? What'll she do, write your letters so you can be scrubbing the floors?"

"Maude, you're impossible. Oh, and don't forget Cook will start Monday. Now, where's Letty?"

"Cleaning the upstairs rooms."

"Good, then I'll bring in the second jug of cider my-self." I went to fetch it before she could complain any more.

I spent the evening going through my wardrobe and sorting out clothing that needed mending and pressing. Still trying to be optimistic about my proposed visit to David Langermann, I wondered what to wear. I finally chose a dark green wool suit with peaked sleeves and a wide collar, which I folded to take downstairs for Maude to press.

The next afternoon, I borrowed Maude's keys and went up to the ballroom. As I put the brass key into the lock and turned it, I felt only apprehensive, my fears much lessened in the light of day. Even with the heavy draperies keeping most of the sun from the large room, there was light enough to see by. I could hear some of Johannes's workmen pounding with hammers outside, and the awareness that there were others about put me even more at ease.

There was nothing here now. My heels echoed on the once lustrous floorboards, and the stage where the or-chestra played was bare. I walked toward the stage warily. But it, too, was thickly covered with dust. To one side, rusty music stands faced the wall. What had I expected to see? Footprints where musicians had played the night before last and then left, through the locked door, taking their instruments with them?

I checked the French doors. They were all latched except for the set Maude had left unlocked that first night. I opened that pair and stepped out onto the bal-cony, proceeding carefully, for Johannes had not yet thoroughly inspected the balcony to make sure it was secure. The stone railing seemed sturdy enough, but still . . .

I looked down into the yard and saw Johannes, in his white shirt and suspendered trousers. He straightened from sawing a piece of lumber, and when he caught my eye I waved to him and he smiled. The scene before me filled me with a sense of well-being, and I decided not to think anymore of ghosts.

On Thursday Amelia arrived. I was downstairs when she drove up in her father's buggy, and I walked out to greet her. She was fetching in a yellow-and-blue-striped dress, trimmed with overskirt and flounces, and a bonnet of navy felt trimmed with a blue feather and yellow ribbon.

"Good morning, *Miss* Erika," she said, as if trying to get used to the formality of her position, but I knew she was teasing me.

"Bring your buggy around back. Pepys will take care of your horse."

"Who's Pepys?"

"He works in the stables." I lowered my voice. "He takes a bit of getting used to. He's a little odd."

"Oh, I think I've seen him. But never mind. I'll be nice to him."

Just outside the stables I found Pepys bending over an old horseshoe. He looked up startled.

"Pepys, I want you to meet someone." Amelia was patting her horse, and she turned and beamed at the shy man as I introduced them.

Amelia said, "I'm glad to meet you, Pepys. This is Lulu." She indicated the mare.

"Yes, ma'am," Pepys said softly. They were the first words I think I'd ever heard him speak. Then he took the reins from her, looped them around a post and began to unhook the buggy.

We soon forgot Pepys and turned to gaze around. "Oh, Erika," said Amelia, "this must be so exciting for you. Imagine, your very own hotel!"

"Humph," I said, placing my hands on my hips. "At the moment it's nothing but a lot of work."

She smiled brilliantly at me. "What will I do first?"

"You can help me tally up the estimates I've got for the masonry." I looked for Johannes and saw him above us on a scaffold. "Do you know Johannes Berglund, the man working on the shutters up there?"

"I've seen him in the village."

"It's his men you see working here." I heaved a sigh. "I just hope they finish in time."

She gazed at Johannes. "He must have very good balance. I'd be scared to death up there."

"I suppose he's had a lot of experience. Let's go in." She followed me.

"We'll set up the office behind the main desk downstairs," I said. "I've had Letty sweep and dust in there. There's only an old rolltop desk and a worktable, but I've ordered some filing cabinets. What color do you think we should paint it?" I asked when we came to the room.

"Well, it's drab in here with no windows. How about light green? Then it would always feel like spring."

"Green would harmonize with the wallpaper I plan to put in this corridor." I nodded thoughtfully. "All right, green it is."

I tried to open the rolltop desk, but couldn't. "I don't even know what's in here," I said. "I'll have to ask Maude for the key. Never mind. We can work on your table here."

We drew up the heavy office chairs and worked all morning. Amelia had an aptitude for figures and made good suggestions. She was even more interested in the work than I'd expected.

We stopped for luncheon, and Maude served us a hearty stew. Afterward we were discussing how best to arrange the furniture in the office when Teddy came in. He'd been to the post office that morning and had brought the mail.

"A letter for you, miss," he said, handing me a large square envelope with deckle edging on the flap and firm handwriting with my name on the front. His brows lowered in a brief frown, and then he left us.

I saw instantly whom it was from, and I sat down, reaching for the letter opener. Amelia looked on curiously.

My heart beat rapidly as I slit the edge of the envelope and began reading. When at last I looked up, Amelia was staring at me expectantly.

"It's from David Langermann." I straightened, not knowing what the girl might have learned about him from her father. "I'm to call on him at my convenience to discuss business. I spoke to your father about this, Amelia. I shall go to see him early next week, but without you, I'm afraid."

"Yes, my father told me I wasn't to go. But, Erika, it's so fascinating. How I would love to meet him!"

"Why?" *Because his father killed my mother?* I wondered. I felt a now-familiar resentment.

"He just seems so mysterious, Erika. Living on his estates alone like that in East Hampton."

"How do you know he lives alone?"

She sat forward, her voice a hushed stage whisper. "Because his father was a murderer, and so he must have become a recluse. But he's probably very handsome and very rich."

I could see that far from being horrified at the prospects of meeting a murderer's son, she found it quite a romantic notion. But her next statement disturbed me.

"Do you think he's mad?"

"Whatever do you mean?"

"The way I heard the story, his father, Gerhard Langermann, went made because your mother tormented him—never forgave him for marrying another woman."

Then she blinked and dropped her gaze. "I'm sorry. It's just that one hears things, you see."

"I wouldn't know what you've heard," I said. "In any case you're not to go with me, I'm afraid. I shall take Maude or Letty."

She sniffed. "Maude won't want to go. And Letty's not trained to be a companion."

"I admit I would enjoy your company, but I've made an agreement with your father, and I intend to keep my word."

"Why not ask Mr. Langermann here instead, so we can see him?"

"It is I who have proposed business to him; therefore it is proper that I should call on him."

"But a gentleman should call on a lady, not vice versa."

"We are . . ." I almost said brother and sister. "We have potential business in common, so it's all right."

She puckered her face, then a thought struck her and she brightened. "If you become partners, then he might come to see you here."

"He might," I admitted.

After that I drafted some letters and Amelia copied them in her neat hand on clean sheets of stationery. Then we organized a bookkeeping system.

At the end of the day I sent Amelia to ask Maude for her keys, and when she returned we tried the rolltop desk but with no luck. I was about to give up in despair, thinking the only way might be to break the lock. It hadn't concerned me much before, for my father's attorneys already had all the important papers in connection with the hotel, and Maude had kept my mother's ledgers together. But now that we couldn't get into the desk, my curiosity was aroused.

"Let me try again," I said, taking the bunch of keys from Amelia. I chose one of the smaller ones we'd tried unsuccessfully earlier and pushed it into the lock. It seemed to fit, and finally the lock gave.

"Here, help me roll the shutter up." Though it wouldn't budge at first, it finally moved, but only halfway.

As I expected, there were some brittle old papers and a bottle of ink that had dried solid. I poked gingerly into the musty cubbyholes, not wanting to come into contact with anything that might have decided to live there.

"There doesn't seem to be much of interest, but I'll clean it out so we can use it." I shut the top and said, "Maude will be getting supper. And I've had Letty make up the room next to mine for you."

After our meal I took Amelia to her room. Like the others, it needed new wall coverings and paint, but the four-poster bed was sturdy and the highboy and dresser quite usable.

"When the busy season opens, I'll have to rent this room to guests and you'll have a room in the servants' quarters, but I thought you might enjoy it here for now."

"Oh, yes, it's very lovely," she said, running her hand along the silky bed coverlet.

"If you like," I said, "we can sit up for a while in my room. You can tell me all about life in the village."

"Oh, yes, let's do sit and talk!"

When we got settled in my sitting room, Amelia mentioned David Langermann's letter. I tried to get her off the subject, but she kept coming back to it. I had thought it wouldn't bother me to talk about the tragedy of my parents' lives, but I found as we sat in the yellow light of the kerosene lamps, that it all came back to me disturbingly afresh.

Amelia was settled deep in the wing chair, and as she spoke, her voice took on a breathless quality, as if the story of my mother and Gerhard Langermann had cast a spell on her.

"They were lovers, weren't they?" she said.

I nodded, and my face reddened, for I felt I was on the verge of learning if anyone else knew I was Gerhard's bastard child, or if my legal father, Edward Barlow, had convinced everyone that I was his.

"My father told me it was sinful," Amelia said. "She should have obeyed her father and made her husband a good wife."

I sighed. "That may be so. I believe my mother married before she was ready to settle down."

"But they had you."

I was afraid to meet her gaze, afraid I would give myself away. "Yes," I said.

But she continued, still caught up in the story. "It was after that, wasn't it? They met one last time at the Hook Windmill near Gerhard's land. And he went mad and strangled her."

Grief I thought I had mastered swept over me as I pictured my mother with her blond hair spread over the floor of the old windmill, a man bent over her. I felt sickened at the thought of my mother's violent death, and my face must have shown something of my emotions, for Amelia leaned forward, her eyes round.

"Does it upset you, Erika? Perhaps we shouldn't be talking of it."

"No," I said, rising to open the window for a bit of fresh air. "I don't want to run away from the truth. I wanted to know what people knew about it."

Suddenly I heard it. My hand froze on the window latch. The music was faint, but it was there. The tinkling sound of the waltz. I looked at Amelia, whose surprised expression told me she heard it, too.

"What is it?" she asked, looking out the window.

"I don't know," I said. "But I've heard it before. So has Maude. Do you believe in ghosts, Amelia?" My voice was tight, my hands cold. I almost hoped she would say no, to persuade me I was dreaming.

But her eyes widened, and she took a step toward me, as she glanced upward at the floor above us. "You mean a spirit," she said, "someone whose body has been buried in a grave, but who can't rest...."

My voice shook as I said, "That's what Maude thinks. She thinks it's my mother."

"Your mother? But it's music. What could it mean?"

"Maude says..." But I stopped, feeling foolish, feeling as if I was only perpetuating a myth.

"Yes?" she prodded me.

"Well, Maude thinks it's because Julie Ann and Gerhard once danced together in the ballroom upstairs. One of the only times she was truly happy."

Her grip on my arm tightened, and I tensed. "Then we must go see," she said.

It was what I had planned, I realized, by putting her in the room next to mine—to see if she would hear the music, too. Yet now that she actually proposed we go to the ballroom, I found myself trembling.

"I'm sure there's nothing to be frightened of," I said aloud, more to reassure myself than Amelia. I picked up one of the lamps and led the way to the door. As I placed my foot on the stairs, the music drifted down again, and Amelia clutched my arm so that I nearly dropped the lamp.

I had kept the key to the ballroom's double doors when I returned the bunch to Maude. If she noticed I'd slipped it off, she had said nothing.

When we reached the fourth floor, we walked toward the double doors. The music seemed louder. I must have been shaking very hard, for when I took the key from my pocket and inserted it in the lock, I nearly dropped it. The key squeaked and turned and finally we pushed the doors open. Perhaps I closed my eyes, for when I opened them, I was aware that the music had stopped.

The draperies over one set of French doors billowed out and moonlight danced over the floor. The door behind us slammed shut and Amelia screamed, then clasped her hand over her mouth.

We stood for some moments, until I realized there was nothing there. The wind had slammed the door. I breathed again.

"Hello," I called out, my own voice making me jump. "Is anyone here? Come," I said to Amelia. "We'll see how the French doors came to be unlatched."

"Are they usually locked?" she whispered, keeping right behind me as I walked across the floor.

"I think so." As we came nearer the stage, I held the lamp higher. There was no one there, no ghostly instrument. I was shaking, but I kept telling myself there was some rational explanation.

I hesitated near the French doors. If there were a burglar on the other side, we might be in danger, for we had no weapon. Still, there were two of us, and I summoned what courage I had left and stepped through the doors onto the balcony.

Nothing happened. I gazed at the three-quarter moon hanging in the misty sky. The shore was not visible, for a fog had rolled in from the beach, but I could hear the lapping waves. There was no one here, and except for the fact that I could not explain the open French doors, there was nothing to be frightened of. Amelia stood beside me, shaking, but as we had found nothing, I turned to go in.

"Do...do you think it could be your mother?" she asked after I had closed and locked the door.

"It's possible," I admitted. "She could be trying to communicate with me..."

We didn't dally in the ballroom, but left quickly, locking the double doors behind us. We made our way downstairs and came to my room. Amelia followed me in again and I can't say I minded the company.

Amelia drew her chair up to the fire, which had burned low. She rubbed her arms. "The music," she said. "It was a waltz, wasn't it?"

"Yes. Only a snatch of it, but always the same. Maude said it was the tune Julie Ann always asked the orchestra to play. It was the one she danced to with Gerhard." I shook my head. "That puzzles me. If they were lovers, I can't imagine that they'd dance together in public. How could they flaunt themselves that way in front of everyone?"

Amelia thought. "Perhaps your mother danced with all the gentlemen. Perhaps Gerhard attended a ball just to show Captain Edward and your grandfather that he had pride, too, and that he could face them in public. If that were the case, then not to have danced together would have been more obvious. Perhaps they danced just once." Amelia lowered her voice. "My father said she was very lovely. She had hair like yours. And Gerhard must have been very handsome."

Thinking of Gerhard made me think of his son, and the reply he had finally sent me. "I shall leave tomorrow for East Hampton."

"Oh, how I should love to go with you!" Amelia said.

I gave her a sympathetic smile, remembering my promise to her father. "I'll have to make do with Letty. I promise to tell you all about it."

She sighed dejectedly as I walked with her to the door. I could see that she was caught up in the unsolved love affair from the past, though somehow her interest made me feel uneasy.

"Perhaps," she said to me, as I held the door for her, "David Langermann can tell you why his father killed Julie Ann."

CHAPTER FIVE

LETTY AND I DROVE in the buggy to the bustling town of Greenport early the next morning and took the ferry crossing. After a brief stop in Sag Harbor for refreshment, we were off again, following the toll road to the town of East Hampton. It grew colder, and the tree branches bowed overhead, like straining fingers entangled above us. I imagined my mother on her last fatal trip along this road. What had driven her to come this far?

Indeed it was a mystery to me how her affair had proceeded after Gerhard had married and moved to the South Fork. I wondered if David Langermann would be able to shed any more light on the subject, if he would even speak of it. I also wondered how he would receive me. His letter had been brief, and I knew it by heart.

My dear Miss Barlow,
Forgive my tardy reply and my reticence to answer. Since you propose to discuss business with me, I suggest you call at Mulgrove House at your convenience.

Yours, David Langermann

It could hardly be said to convey warmth. And he didn't explain his reticence, only admitted he had some. I was feeling more and more ashamed of my overactive curiosity. David Langermann had most likely buried his father's past and had perhaps been quite shocked to hear from me.

Finally we reached the outskirts of East Hampton. We turned onto Main Street, where tapering poplars bordered the expanse of the wide road. My hands were weary of holding the reins, for even the kid gloves I wore could not prevent the soreness from clutching the reins all day. I pulled up to ask directions to Mulgrove House.

As I entered a little shop, a bell tinkled overhead, and a woman smiled at me from behind a counter laden with bolts of cloth. "Good afternoon," she said. "May I help you?"

"I'm afraid I need directions." I showed her the paper on which David Langermann had roughly sketched the roads leading to Mulgrove House.

"Yes," said the woman, bending over the paper. "Now I recognize it."

She pointed east. "At the next crossing, take the road south for a mile. You'll see the dunes ahead, where the road ends." She consulted the sketch again. "There's another turnoff here. The house is well hidden."

I thanked her and returned to the buggy. Turning off the main road we drove past fields cultivated with strawberry plants. The sky had turned leaden now, making it appear much darker than it really was. Bordering the fields were lopped trees that grew horizontally to form a living fence with adjacent trees.

The air was heavy with the threat of rain. I peered to our right, hoping we had not passed the last turnoff and was relieved to see a small road leading into the woods again. There was no sign, but there appeared to be no other road ahead, only the dunes.

The wind came up then and the bays began tossing their heads. I urged them forward into the woods, and soon with the thick cover, it was quite dark. The road kept doubling back, and as we rounded yet another bend, the horses balked and whinnied. Peering ahead, I saw that there was a large branch across the road.

"Hold the reins, Letty," I said over the wind and got down to see if it would budge. I took hold of some of the prickly branches and was able to move it only a little.

"I need your help," I shouted to Letty. She tied the reins and came to help me. It started to rain, but we made our way around the branch, and using all our strength, managed to get it out of the way. The dampness irritated me, and having to deal with the obstruction in our path put me in a bad temper. *He could at least have kept his roads clear,* I thought as we climbed back into the buggy.

At last the trees parted on a verdant lawn that led down to a pond. A thick hedge rose beyond that, with a stone fence behind. Half-hidden by trees was a dark, gabled mansion. Mulgrove House was scarcely visible at all except when lightning slashed across the sky, illuminating the leaded-glass windowpanes.

The gravel drive took us through a stone arch, and suddenly we were before the front door. I had Letty hold the reins again, while I ran up the steps and lifted the heavy brass knocker and banged on the door. A brilliant flash of lightning lit up the whole countryside, followed by a loud crack of thunder, which made the horses rear. I ran back to grab their bridles when the door opened, and a thin woman, not much older than I was, dressed in black silk and white apron, emerged on the steps.

"God in heaven," she said in a thick German accent, coming down the steps toward me. "You'll catch your death of cold." She had to shout above the storm, but I was afraid to let go of the horses. Much to my relief a young man in a black cap, leather vest and riding boots came around the house and took charge of the horses.

The woman hustled Letty and me inside. As we stood dripping in the entryway, I pulled from my pocket the wet piece of paper that had been David's letter.

"I'm Erika Barlow," I said. "I'm sorry if we've arrived at an inopportune time, but I've come from the North Fork to see Mr. Langermann."

"I'm Mrs. Hanson, the housekeeper. Take off your jackets or you'll catch a chill. You'd better wait in here where there's a fire."

She showed me into a large room with a huge stone fireplace where a warm fire blazed. Most of the furniture was heavy mahogany and leather, and with the bearskin rug on the floor the room had a distinctly masculine quality. A large gold-colored tufted wing chair was drawn up to the fire, and I crossed to sit there while Mrs. Hanson took Letty to the kitchen.

When I heard the door open, I half expected my host to appear, but it was the housekeeper again. "I've sent for some hot tea, and a room is being made up for you. You'll stay the night, of course."

"Oh, I . . . I had intended to stay at the inn in town."

"You won't be going there now, and Mr. Langermann would insist."

"I suppose you're right about not being able to travel. I do need to get these wet things off. Have you informed Mr. Langermann I am here?"

"This I cannot do, for he is not at home."

"Not home?" My heart sank.

She shook her head. "He has gone to his business."

"Do you mean the lace factory in Patchogue?"

"Yes, miss." She frowned, and I saw lines in her face that indicated she was older than I had first thought, yet her expression was not completely unfriendly.

"Then he is likely to be gone several days."

"Perhaps you will wait. He will return tomorrow or the next day."

I sighed. "I suppose I shall have to wait. If it will not be too much trouble, that is."

"No trouble. Would you like to go to your room?"

"Yes, certainly." There was no point waiting down here any longer when I could have the benefit of dry clothes upstairs.

"Shall I send your maid to help you unpack? Otto will have your luggage up by now."

"No, I'll unpack. I've not brought much." I presumed Otto was the butler.

As she led me up a wide flight of stairs, I glanced higher at the exposed beams and at the double-arched window on the landing we approached. When the lightning flashed outside the leaded-glass panes, I could see the trees and shrubbery below.

We passed along a wainscoted hallway, and she opened the door to a bedroom also furnished with heavy mahogany pieces; the bed hangings were a deep red, and fire blazed in the hearth.

She left me, and I stood before the fire warming myself. I felt dejected. The cold damp ride from East Hampton had done nothing to improve my spirits. David Langermann could have said in his letter that he would be away, for he'd asked me to call at my convenience. Now I would be cooped up here waiting at least another day. I angrily tugged the pins from my hair, letting it fall about my shoulders, then I unlaced and removed my kid boots and extracted my quilted dressing gown from my case. There was a knock on the door and Otto brought a tray of food, which he set on a low table.

"Would you like anything else, miss?" he inquired after he had uncovered the steaming dishes.

"No, thank you. This looks delicious."

The food tasted as good as it looked, and with the wood crackling in the fireplace and the storm raging outside, I began to feel more cozy. After eating, I leaned back in the snug wing chair and watched the flames dance in front of me. I closed my eyes and dozed off.

A tumbling log brought my head up with a jerk. I hadn't meant to fall asleep. When I stood up to poke the dying fire, I noticed the tray was gone. Otto must have come in, seen me asleep and removed it without disturbing me.

After getting the blaze going again, I walked to my window and pushed the draperies aside; it was quite dark now, and there was no moon. My nap had revived me, and I was no longer sleepy, so I considered going to the library, which I had earlier seen off the downstairs hallway. I felt restless and thought I might enjoy browsing through the books. Besides, my innate curiosity made me want to see what sort of books David Langermann kept in his library, for could you not judge a man by what he liked to read?

I reached for the bellpull to let Mrs. Hanson know where I was going, then I thought better of it. I had no idea of the time, and it would be silly to wake up the household just to tell them I was going to the library when I could easily find my way alone.

I wrapped my dressing gown securely around me, buttoning it to the throat. I lit the kerosene lamp that sat on the table by my chair, then went out into the darkened hallway. The rain still pattered on the windowpanes, and I could hear the wind whistling in the rafters. I saw by the hands of the tall clock at the bottom of the stairs that it was past two o'clock.

I proceeded toward the library. The door was closed now, but I grasped the large brass doorknob and turned it. The door opened with a creak, and I entered, closing it behind me. I lit another lamp, and soon the room was illumined with a soft glow.

Bookshelves covered two walls. Above the large marble fireplace on the far wall was a painting of a man in his late twenties with a narrow face, dark hair and eyes that gazed somberly into the distance. He wore a black frock coat with dark cravat.

I walked closer, tilting my head to study the brushstrokes, for I thought the artist had caught something of the man's resignation and pain. His hands rested on the back of a leather armchair, and I looked at the long fingers with morbid curiosity. These were the hands that had caressed my mother—graceful hands, almost delicate for a man, but long enough to wrap around her slender throat.

I went to the bookshelves, running my fingers over the titles. Histories, the classics, also works in French and books on politics. I was bending down to read the titles on a lower shelf when I heard the door creak behind me.

I gasped and whirled around, flattening myself against the bookcase, my hands splayed against the books. My heart was in my throat as I faced the man who stood silhouetted in the door. I could not find my voice, and he did not speak either, as he stood there, only faintly illumined by the lamp I had left on a small table.

Even before I saw his face, I felt a sense of recognition that must have come from our shared blood. I had spent much time imagining what David Langermann would be like, but I had neglected to consider how I might feel when facing the man who was the son of my mother's lover, my own half brother.

He moved with ease as he silently shut the door behind him and stepped into the light, and the awareness that sprang between us was startling. It was like seeing one's own soul transposed into another body.

I was fascinated by his dark eyes, his thick, dark hair, broad shoulders and slim waist. He was dressed in a black wool frock coat, and his white stand-up collar was tied with a dark cravat. I dropped my eyes to the floor and a strange heat warmed my cheeks, but I did not want our meeting to be an uncomfortable one, so I forced myself to look into his eyes again.

He spoke then, his voice deep and musical. "I apologize for startling you," he said. "I was not aware that you were here."

"I'm sorry. I couldn't sleep, and . . ." I paused, then moved a few steps toward the center of the room. My hand unconsciously moved to my throat as I pulled my dressing gown closer around me.

He studied my face intently, then took my hand in a warm grasp. We stood for some seconds, neither one speaking, our hearts frozen in time until the ticking of the clock on the mantel and the hushed patter of rain outside forced themselves into our consciousness.

He dropped my hand and turned to a cabinet that stood to one side of the room. "Some port?" he asked as he lifted a cut-glass carafe and removed the crystal stopper.

At my nod, he filled two glasses with the dark red liquid and said, "Forgive me for not being here when you arrived." I stared at his long slender fingers as they held the glass—graceful, like his father's in the portrait.

He handed me a glass, and I looked quickly away, wondering if he knew what I had been thinking.

"We have not introduced ourselves," he said. "But I presume you know who I am." He continued after he had taken a sip from his glass, "And I believe I know who you are."

"Yes," I said. "Forgive me. I am not yet over my surprise. I am Erika Barlow." *Your sister,* I almost said.

"I knew that." He walked toward the mantel and rested one arm on it as he turned back to me. "Your letter was unexpected."

My face flushed, and I felt doubly self-conscious facing him in my state of undress. The warmth that had emanated from him when he had first seen me had diminished and was replaced by a half-sardonic expression, and all my doubts about the wisdom of meeting him flooded over me at once.

"I should not have come," I said, not really meaning to speak aloud as I set my glass on an end table. As if sensing my desire to flee, he crossed the room and reached out his hand to cover mine as I started to remove it from the glass.

But his grasp did more than stop me. I felt a warm pulse pass between us that was almost frightening. I tried to tell myself that the feeling that sprang between us was the natural result of our being related, but still I was unprepared for it. The touch of our hands intensified the spark I had already felt at a distance from him.

Something flashed in his eyes. Some struggle was going on inside him, as well. He started to move toward me, then he dropped my hand and lifted his chin.

"Don't leave," he said. "At least let's talk."

I teetered on the edge of leaving, but now that he had let go of me, I could think more rationally.

"Please," he said. "Sit down." He indicated the leather chair with the nailhead trim beside the table, and I realized that it was the same chair as in the painting of his father. I moved unsteadily around it and sat.

He poured himself another glass of port and drank from it, then he lit a match to some kindling in the fireplace. In a minute, the flame licked the dry logs. I sat stone still as he turned to face me again.

"You are wondering about me," he said, the sardonic expression in his eyes again, "as I have wondered about you."

My mouth jerked in a nervous twitch. "Then you know about me."

"My mother didn't tell me anything about you at first." He brushed a hand through his hair and then stared up at the portrait of his father. "She only told me that my father never really loved her."

I shook my head in sympathy, but I didn't speak.

"As I grew up I heard the whisperings among the servants. Then in school as a boy it was hard to avoid the taunts. I was the son of a murderer, after all."

"I'm sorry," I whispered, looking at my lap, my hair falling forward over my shoulders.

"I grew used to it," he said.

I imagined what he must have suffered. He watched me, and again I was aware of the closeness between us.

But I hoped he would not come near me again. I could barely tolerate the intensity of shared feelings that ran between us at this distance.

"When I was older," he continued, "I demanded that my mother tell me *why* he didn't love her. She had not really meant to tell me that in the first place, you see; she had only admitted it in a moment of bitterness."

He walked toward me again, studying my face. Then he reached out to touch my chin, slowly lifting my face to better examine it in the firelight.

"She said my father had always loved another woman, that she was beautiful and very fair, but that they had been forbidden to marry because of their parents' prejudices. My mother knew this, for my father had told her the truth when he asked her to marry him. He wanted her to know everything, but he swore he would try to make a good husband and father."

"And she could accept that?"

"He was kind to her, even though he was still in love with Julie Ann Barlow." He laughed harshly, dropping his hand and looking at the portrait once again. "I used to hate him for leaving my mother so saddened, for being mad enough to strangle a woman." He shrugged. "There was nothing I could do to help her, you see..."

"It must have been hard for you."

He turned to stare at me, his dark eyes seeming to press me back against my seat. "I learned that with passion came pain. I knew that I had to be stronger than he was. I had to turn my back on all of it and make my own life."

My heart felt cold, knowing that instead of growing up in the midst of a loving family, he had grown up with only pain and regret surrounding him. No wonder he had closed himself in this dark house in the dark woods. He'd felt little love from his mother, almost none from a father who had been taken from him when he was but a child. And he had witnessed great sadness in his mother, whose husband had been driven mad by the passion of another woman. So he had shut himself off from the emotion called love and replaced it with bitterness.

And yet I had felt a natural warmth in him when we first set eyes on each other. There was something about his expression, as if he would thank the person who had the strength to pull away the mask he wore.

He gestured with the hand that held his glass. "I do not spend all my time here. I have business interests that keep me away. And I spend much time in London and Paris."

"So far away?"

He smiled. "Far enough away that my father's reputation is of no import. Abroad I am welcomed in many circles of society, especially by impoverished nobility who hope I will marry one of their daughters."

"I see." I should have been relieved to know that he got some enjoyment out of life after all, that he did not always cloister himself here. But something pulled at me when I thought that he had to cross the ocean to seek enjoyment, to escape his identity here.

"And what of you?" he asked suddenly.

"What do you mean?" I said.

He lifted the carafe to refill my glass. "You have come to see me about your hotel. But is that not just an excuse? Did you not want to see for yourself the heir of your mother's lover?"

I turned my head aside, resenting the malice in his tone. He was taunting me, perhaps taking out on me some of the pent-up hostility he had suffered from others.

But he was right about my curiosity. As to our true relationship, our blood relationship, I still did not know for certain what he knew. He had said our parents were lovers, but not that my father was his.

"I admit to being curious. I am sorry if it is upsetting to you."

"If your mother had half your beauty, I cannot blame my father for what he did."

He said this without malice, and I could only stare at him, shocked to the very depths of my being.

He moved nearer, but this time his nearness did not frighten me as it had before. His look was vulnerable as he lifted a strand of my hair, gold in the firelight.

"Her hair was the same color," he said. Then when he met my eyes, he dropped my hair and turned back to the fireplace. I sat trembling. He rubbed the back of his neck with his hand, and I grasped the arms of my chair, resisting the urge I had to reach out and touch his other hand. I was disturbed by my reactions, for I could not sort out my intense feelings.

"You had a natural curiosity about your sibling," he said.

I swallowed hard, the blood coursing through my veins. "Then you know."

"Forgive me if what I say is indelicate," he said.

He poured himself more sherry, perhaps to calm himself, for I could see the tenseness in the muscles about his neck. "But between ourselves, we must be honest about our..." He paused, raising the glass. "Our relationship."

"Yes." A tightness clenched my jaw and stomach. Still I knew we must clear the air. We had to say it. "Our blood relationship."

He swirled the red liquid in his glass, then tossed it back as I lowered my eyes. I had just admitted to him that I was his bastard sister. Shame filled me, and yet there was something about our secret that strangely excited me.

"How do you know of my—" I couldn't meet his gaze "—parentage?"

I heard the clink of his glass on the silver tray. "My mother claimed that my father told Julie Ann he would not see her again, but that Julie Ann implored him to meet her. In the end, he killed her, for she would give him no peace." He turned and walked slowly toward the fireplace. "Julie Ann had a child. Some said the child was my father's."

"And yet," I said morosely, "my legal father, Edward Barlow, said I was his, and he made my mother face society."

"Of course. To salvage her reputation."

I shook my head piteously. "How they must have laughed behind her back."

"Most likely." He said this last gently, and I felt his sympathy now. He was not taunting as he had been before.

I told him that I had gone to live with my aunt in Maine, that the hotel had been left to me in trust until this year—that I wanted to try my hand at the business.

"I find," I said at last, "that the hotel needs a great deal of refurbishing after standing empty for twenty years." My stomach muscles tightened. I reminded myself that I wasn't asking for charity; I was looking for a business partner.

When I finished, he raised his brows and nodded in indication that he had heard my request and was considering it. I glanced toward the windows and could perceive the faint beginning of light in the sky. David's eyes were heavy, and he held a hand to his mouth to stifle a yawn.

"I'm afraid I'm in no condition to carry this discussion further," he said. "Perhaps we should retire and talk later today." He pulled his mouth back in a teasing expression. "It might be well if you retired to your room, for should the servants find you thus..."

A dark brow raised, he let his eyes drift over me, and though for some time I had forgotten the way I was dressed, so engrossed was I in our discussion, now he made me uncomfortably aware of my state. I rose, the blush coming to my cheeks again.

"Of course," I said. "It is very late."

He went to the window and cranked it open, and a rush of fresh air came into the room. Smells of the ocean mixed with the damp left from the storm.

"Did you travel in the rain?" I asked.

"I'm afraid so. I had meant to put up at the inn at Good Ground when the storm worsened, but the place was full, so I waited until the worst had passed and pushed on. My carriage is very secure from the elements, though I'm sorry to say my driver got the worst of it."

"I'm glad you arrived safely," I said.

He escorted me to the door. "Thank you." His eyes held tenderness in them for a moment as if he were glad I cared about his welfare. Then he opened the door and shielded his look with formal courtesy.

"Good night, Erika," he said.

"Good night." I swallowed. My name on his lips sounded natural, and yet I could not bring myself to say his.

I made my way up to my room, my mind in a daze. Soon the comfort of the sheets drawn around me and the chirping of birds lulled me to sleep.

CHAPTER SIX

I AWOKE TO A MORNING refreshed by the rain. I donned a cream wool suit and pinned my hair in coils at the back of my head. I was just finishing my toilet when there was a knock on my door.

"Mr. Langermann wanted to know if you would have breakfast with him in the dining room," Mrs. Hanson said upon entering.

"Thank you, I will."

Downstairs, she took me to the east wing of the house. The large dining room had a baronial-size dining table and high-backed chairs. A sideboard held silver-covered dishes, and Otto was pouring coffee from an ornate silver coffee urn. David put his newspaper aside and rose when he saw me.

"I trust you rested well," he said.

"That I did."

Otto held a chair for me. I wondered if David always breakfasted with such formality, and I had to hide my amusement as I thought of the casual, hearty breakfasts Cook prepared for us in the hotel kitchen, where I usually sat with Maude, Teddy, Letty and Johannes, if he arrived early for his day's work.

"You have a lovely home, David," I said, forcing myself to use his given name.

He smiled, catching my eye and holding it. "I hope you find it comfortable." His look made me somehow nervous, and I concentrated on the food.

Otto served me a plate of fluffy eggs and fried potatoes, and I relished the food, taking two cups of strong coffee. By the time I had finished breakfast, my spirits were high. David seemed in a pleasant mood as well and suggested a ride to the dunes.

I changed into a skirt and jacket I could use to ride sidesaddle, and David met me in the downstairs hall, wearing a tweed hunting jacket and high black leather boots.

The horses were ready, and I mounted a dun-colored mare; David's mount was a roan. We set off on a path that led through thick brambles and cranberry bogs. At last we came out of the thick undergrowth to the edge of the barren dunes. Here low scrub mingled with sand, and David led us where the footing was fairly secure, though moist from the previous night's rain. I could hear the waves rushing to shore on the other side of the rise.

"Come," David said. The horses seemed to know the way down the path away from the ocean. We entered a wooded area where the roar of the waves suddenly seemed far away. It was colder here out of the sun, and the undergrowth thicker. At last we came to a clearing, and I glanced up in surprise. A small moss-covered cottage of split shingles stood half-hidden before us.

"My father's hunting lodge," David said, and leading me to it, he dismounted, came around to help me down and then tied the horses to a nearby tree. I followed him into the cottage.

I did not expect such a place to boast any amenities, but was surprised to enter a large room with a freshly swept hearth. A rough wooden table and two chairs sat on one side. There was a gun rack on one wall, with weapons that looked ready to use.

"My father liked to shoot," David said as he walked to the hearth and inspected the kindling. He knelt and lit a fire.

"David," I said as we stood spreading our hands before the blaze. "I think perhaps it was wrong of me to come here." I struggled for words, made all the harder by his nearness, for when he stood close to me I could feel his energy, and I was aware of the blood rushing through my veins.

"I realize I wanted to know more about..." I hesitated. "About our past. But I have decided it cannot do us any good, thinking of people who are beyond the grave."

He raised his hands then and touched my shoulder, turning me to face him so that I looked into his intense dark eyes. "Erika, you cannot deny that their blood runs in our veins."

My eyes widened at the intensity of his look. I had felt sorry for him, thinking of him as a bitter recluse, turning to the gayer side of life in Europe, where his looks and money gave him the chance to forget the stigma he was under at home. But now I felt frightened, knowing that he had repressed much anger and pain and that it was likely to burst forth in him.

"Oh, God," I said, feeling faint. "What have I done?"

Indeed my knees began to give way, but he guided me to a chair, into which I slumped. He left me there, my head in my hands, and I heard him moving about and rattling pans. In a few minutes he had placed a steaming mug of tea before me.

I sipped it, drawing strength. When I finally looked at him again, he was standing thoughtfully before the hearth, his collar pulled up around his neck.

"Are you feeling better?" he asked.

"Yes. Thank you for the tea."

"Erika," he said, "please don't let me frighten you. I thought that you of all people might understand me." He paused. "Surely you must know there are few people I can talk to."

"I...I think I understand." Besides my feelings of accord with him, I could truly understand the desire to throw off the fetters of the past, to not be constantly reminded of the shame of one's family.

"Do you yourself not have unanswered questions?" he asked, turning to me. "Have you not pondered your mother's fate?" He looked into my eyes, and though I did not answer, he nodded.

"I thought so," he said. He went to the wooden chair opposite me and placed a booted foot on the lower rung, gripping the chair back with his hands.

"Tell me," he said.

I closed my eyes. He was right. I, too, had been driven by a quest for the truth, to seek answers to questions that others had long ago buried.

"There is music," I began. I was not looking at him, but I heard him exhale a breath as I went on, "Not always, but sometimes at night. It comes from above, from the ballroom, but when I go up, there is nothing there."

"What does the music sound like?"

"It is a waltz. Only snatches, but it is something my mother used to enjoy dancing to, I believe. It has a low, tinkling sound, like bells, or a music box."

His face seemed to drain of color. "The tune?"

"I do not sing well, but it's something like this." I attempted to hum a phrase.

He stood up straight, suddenly staring at me, and I stopped abruptly.

"What is it?" I asked.

He took a deep breath and walked to the center of the room. "Never mind," he said. "We've been gone quite a time," he added, "we should be returning."

"Very well." I rose, and he came toward me. We stood face-to-face for some seconds and I was aware of the pounding of my heart. His eyes held mine, and when I tried to back away, he took hold of my arms, preventing me from moving.

I could not believe what was happening. Suddenly, he brought me very near him, and when he lifted a hand to brush my cheek with his fingers, I couldn't move. His fingers found their way into my hair, and as his hand rested on the back of my neck, he breathed my name. I dropped my gaze to his mouth.

"Erika," he said again, his lips moving closer.

"No," I whispered, and then I felt his hand move in my hair. I knew it was wrong, but I wanted to wind my arms about his neck. The blood pounded in my ears, and I averted my face.

But he turned my face back to his and brought his mouth to mine. Emotions churned in my breast, the sensation spreading through me like flames fanned by the wind. When he released my mouth, I gasped for breath.

"David," I breathed. Still he stared down at me, and I could not meet the intensity of emotion in his eyes. He dropped his hands and stepped to the fireplace.

As he put out the fire, I went out of doors, still shaking, glad of the sharp air that helped clear my head. For

I could not believe the confused sensations coursing through me. When at length David emerged from the cottage, we did not speak, only mounted our horses and set off.

When we reached the house I felt relieved, finding the presence of others and the routine of the household somehow reassuring, as if the scene in the cottage had never happened.

David led me into the drawing room, and I brought up the subject of the hotel.

"Have you estimated the costs of running the place once it is refurbished?" he asked.

"Yes. I have brought my figures with me."

"Very well. I will see them after luncheon—though I must tell you I am doubtful about the proposition. And the place is filled with such bad memories for you. Would you not be better off selling?"

"And do what? Work in some factory or hire myself out to someone who does own their own place?"

I saw the smirk on his face and I knew he was laughing at me, but I continued, "I wanted this chance to make my own way. Surely you can understand that."

"After lunch then," he said. "We will meet in my study and go over the figures."

I nodded, feeling that I had at least won a small battle. I repaired to my room to change back into my cream wool suit and brush the tangles from my hair. When I was again presentable, I went downstairs for lunch.

David had changed into a gray serge lounge coat. I took a glass of sherry, which revived me, and we were seated. As we dined on pheasant I asked him to tell me of London and Paris. His face relaxed when he spoke, as if thinking of holidays abroad helped him forget the shadows that hovered over him here. But eventually he came to the subject of his house, asking my opinion of the decor, which he was thinking of changing.

I made some suggestions about wallpaper that might brighten up the rooms, and though he listened intently, I said, "Forgive me. Perhaps you like some of the rooms as they are. I was only thinking that some light and color would add life. It does not seem the sort of place that children would run freely about."

He raised a brow at me. "I have no children."

"But you might someday."

His eyes flashed, and I saw the veiled look that I was sure hid his innermost emotions. "I shall never marry."

"Why not?" Then I clamped my mouth shut, but the words were already out.

As he fixed me with his gaze, a shiver like the one I had felt when he had seized my shoulders at the cottage ran through me. "How can I pass on my family name to innocent children? Besides, what woman would marry a man whose father murdered the woman he loved?"

"But the crime is not inherited," I said. I could not bring myself to speak of the madness.

He shrugged. "All that matters is what others think."

I felt an uncomfortable dryness in my throat and asked for more sherry. It saddened me that David would be the end of his line, and yet I was glad he was not married. Perhaps, I told myself, because I could more easily discuss our business concerns without having to worry about the opinions of a wife.

We were silent for some moments, and then he scraped back his chair and rose. "Shall we go over your proposal in my study?"

"Yes. I will fetch the papers."

He accompanied me to the door. "The study is just there," he said, pointing to another heavy, carved door at the rear of the hallway.

Within five minutes I had returned downstairs with my sheaf of papers, which I carried in a leather portfolio. I handed them to David, and while he sat studying them behind his large oak desk, I let my gaze wander around the room, which was on the order of the library, only smaller.

After a while, David laid the papers aside and reached for a meerschaum pipe that sat nearby. "Do you mind if I smoke?"

"No, I enjoy the smell of pipe tobacco. And my proposal," I said, "have you reached any conclusions?"

He took his time answering, concentrating on getting his pipe lit first. He rose, puffed on the pipe and paced in front of the desk.

"It is a well-founded proposition. As you have pointed out, the number of people visiting Long Island on holiday has increased considerably in the past few years. If a place such as Block Island, which one must reach by ferry, can support eighteen hotels, your idea that Orient Point can support another hotel besides the Orient Inn has merit."

I breathed in relief. Surely I had done a presentable job with my figures to have captured his interest even to this degree.

"The decision is a difficult one, you must admit," he went on. "I am not nearly so ready to confront our—" he lifted an eyebrow "—ghosts. I admire you for meeting the challenge head-on, Erika."

"Thank you," I said stiffly, not knowing where this was leading.

"More perhaps than I. Let me ask you this. Are you looking for a business partner in the fullest sense? One who would advise about the management of the hotel? Or merely a silent partner."

"I had envisioned a silent partner. Of course, the benefit of your business experience would not be unwelcome." My response sounded formal, I knew. But in fact I did not think I would be comfortable working closely with David. He had a way of throwing me off, even when I was doing my utmost to sound agreeable at this stage of our negotiations.

David nodded. "I do not see myself in the role of hotel manager. My time is sewn up with my other affairs. But if I decide that the hotel is a sound investment I would expect reports on the profit and loss, say, twice yearly."

"Then you have not yet decided?"

"You must understand that not all my assets are liquid. I cannot do better than to say that personal feelings aside, the business proposition is a sound one."

"But in this case personal feelings have something to do with it?"

"I'm afraid so." His hand had strayed to a small ornate box that was on the mantel behind his desk where he now stood.

I had not noticed the box before, but as he fingered it, I saw that it was a carved wooden music box. David opened it, and a small porcelain figurine of a woman in a full skirt began to turn to the tinkling music.

David watched me as the notes played. I stared at him dumbfounded as a strange light came into his eyes. I felt suddenly light-headed, as if David and I had somehow left our bodies to float and meet in the middle of the room, turning and turning to that haunting music—the same music that played in the ballroom.

As the music played and David held my gaze, I had the fleeting notion that history in some way was fated to repeat itself.

I became filled with fear. I could not breathe, and though I wanted to escape, my limbs refused to move. I saw that David had felt the same incestuous attraction for me as I had for him. It was impossible not to admit it. He had kissed me in the cottage earlier. Ought not that have been enough to bring me to my senses?

My breath came in short gasps, and I backed away as he moved toward me. I bumped into a chair and tried to step around it, but I was too late, for he had reached me, and his hands grasped my shoulders.

Had my mind succeeded in sending the proper messages to my body I could have slipped away from him, but it did not. His face was only inches from mine as I bent backward against the chair, desperately fighting what was about to happen. Still the music played on, and I thought I would go mad.

"Erika," he said. "Do you understand now why I cannot do as you ask? Do you not see?"

I moved my head from side to side. "No, no," I whispered, denying that this was happening. But all the while my body was savoring his nearness. My arms were reaching for him as if to acknowledge the feeling of oneness we shared. I had never felt such torture.

"No, David, no," I said, as his arms slipped to my waist. "This cannot happen." I buried my head in his shoulder in a sob, but it was too late. His arms came around me and his mouth found mine, and I parted my lips as they met his. As one of his hands pressed me closer, the fingers of his other rose to my throat to loosen the fastening there. His mouth left mine to plant kisses on my ear and neck.

I could not breathe, and my head was thrown back so that while my mind screamed warnings to stop, I arched toward him. At last I found the strength to stop before it was too late, and I twisted under him, slumping into the chair.

He stood before me, his fists clenched. As I panted for breath he seemed to gather strength against the on-slaught of emotions. He quickly crossed the room and slammed the music box shut.

I leaned against the chair back, still gasping for air, and I saw that he had buried his head in his arm on the mantel.

"No," I whispered to myself, still shaking. I moved to the door, and quickly opening it, left the room.

In the hallway I found Otto and told him I would need my carriage. Then I sent for Letty, threw my bags onto the bed and began packing. I could not stay here another night. I did not understand what was happen-ing between David and myself. Perhaps we were vic-tims of the same curse that had befallen our parents. But I knew Maude had been right. I should never have come here. I should never have opened this door to the insidious secret carried in our blood, in our very makeup. I could not deny it. I felt desire. Desire for a man I knew to be my own half brother. It was too hor-rible to contemplate.

There was a knock at my door, and Mrs. Hanson en-tered. "I understand you are leaving," she said.

"Yes, yes," I stammered. "Mr. Langermann and I have concluded our business."

"Very well."

She did not point out the oddity of the hour I had chosen to leave. Since it was afternoon, I would not make the ferry crossings before nightfall. And it would be unwise for a woman traveling with her maid to be on the roads at night.

Mrs. Hanson left me, and I finished packing. Otto appeared to carry my bags downstairs, and I wondered if he and his wife knew who I was? Did they question my being here or my hasty departure?

David did not appear as my buggy was brought around and loaded, and I turned to thank Mrs. Hanson for her hospitality while Letty waited by the buggy. But as I crossed the drive, I heard David's tread on the steps. He dismissed the servants and came to the buggy. I straightened, determined to reveal nothing of my tumultuous feelings.

His face was a mask as he bowed. He spoke in a voice so low the words barely reached my ears, and I did not miss the irony in his voice. "Goodbye then, dear sister."

I was jolted by an icy feeling that ran down my spine. I knew at that instant that it would be better if we never met again.

"Goodbye." I placed my foot on the step and I felt his hand on my elbow as he helped me into the carriage. I shrank from his touch.

I took up the reins and urged the horses forward. I knew I must look foolish running away like this, and I thought there must be something diabolical about David for him to be able to acknowledge the attraction between us.

He had not precisely replied to my request that he invest in the hotel, but I knew the answer. We could never be business partners.

CHAPTER SEVEN

I WAS RELIEVED when Mulgrove House disappeared from view, for I desperately wanted to put as much distance between us as I could.

"We'll stay at the hotel in Sag Harbor," I told Letty after we'd traveled only a hour or so. I knew she would wonder why we had gone such a short distance before stopping, so I added, "I want to see how the hotel here compares to the accommodations I plan to offer my guests on the North Fork."

The hotel had comfortable quarters. We took our meal in the room and then sat in front of the fire for an hour. Letty mended one of my petticoats and I attempted to read, but the warmth of the fire and the fullness of my stomach lulled me. I was grateful to crawl between the sheets and fall asleep.

The next day we retraced our route from Sag Harbor and finally took the north ferry to Greenport. After the isolation of Mulgrove House, I appreciated the populated town of Greenport where the fishing fleets were busy and trade was brisk along the main streets of town.

I watched a group of fishermen arranging their nets and became aware of one of the men looking at me. He was slouched against the pilings, a battered hat shadowing his face. It was unnerving, but I decided he was just being idly curious, and after a few more minutes, we drove on.

The night's rest had done much to improve my state of mind, and the peaceful surroundings and wide stretch of water as we approached Orient Harbor made me feel sane again.

I had thought David Langermann and I might have something in common, that perhaps because of our blood relation he would understand what motivated me to run the hotel. But I found to my horror that David and I uncannily understood each other all too well, and the final irony was our attraction to each other as man and woman.

Our hotel was a welcome sight. The carpenters had repaired the porch and had torn out the rotting shingles from the roof and were putting in new ones. The boards had been removed from the windows and a great deal of scraping and hammering was going on. I pulled the buggy around the back, and Maude came out of the kitchen, wiping her hands on her apron.

"Well, so you've returned," she said as we got down.

I was sure she guessed something of what had happened between David and me but I put off discussion with her for the time being. Teddy helped me carry my things in, and I was grateful to be left in my room alone to relax before supper.

That evening I ate in the kitchen with Maude and Teddy and told them that I had found David Langermann strangely reclusive, yet evidently a successful businessman. Sure Maude could read my face, I did not meet her glance. For how could I admit that her fears were correct, that the curse of the lovers still hung over our heads?

"He could make no commitment to helping me with the hotel as his assets are tied up at present," I said. "In the meantime, I suppose I should see about getting the money from a bank.''

Teddy raised and lowered his bushy eyebrows. ''You might try the bank in Greenport. I reckon they'll give you the money.''

''Old man Grant left his share of the business to his son,'' Maude added. ''He'll be less likely to be influenced by old tales, if you understand.''

After supper I ensconced myself in my downstairs office, which now had a fresh coat of light green paint. I managed to get the small cast-iron stove going to warm up the room, then lost myself in paperwork. By the time the fire burned low, I had put all my papers away and was ready to go to bed. Taking a kerosene lamp with me, I ascended to my room.

In the morning, Amelia burst in on me as I was just tugging at the lid to the rolltop desk. It seemed to have jammed again, and I was trying to see what was keeping it from rolling all the way back.

''Tell me everything,'' she said as she swept in, her face crimson from the cold air. She removed her bonnet and gloves and warmed her hands over the stove, her eyes sparkling.

I shook my head. ''I'm afraid you're going to be disappointed.''

She looked up, surprised. ''Why, is he ugly? I can't believe he would be ugly.''

I sat back in my chair, letting the desktop fall again. ''He is not ugly. Quite the contrary.''

''Oh, then do tell me about it. Was he fascinating?''

I found it difficult to answer her ebullient questions, especially with my own misgivings about having sought out David.

"He is reclusive," I said. "He manages his lands and his manufacturing company on Long Island and takes long holidays abroad."

"Then he must be wealthy," Amelia said.

"It would seem so, but I am afraid he hasn't much capital just now for an investment. So you will not be seeing him."

Amelia's face fell. I felt unreasonably irritated with her, wanting to get off the subject. I rose and tapped a list I had put on her writing table. "But I have a project I think you will enjoy."

"Yes?"

"There are many fine paintings here in the hotel. I want to inventory them and decide which ones need restoring or cleaning. Then, after the inventory, I might have them appraised."

"Oh, that is a good idea. Will we do it now?"

"Yes. We'll begin in the dining room and the lounge."

She seemed to forget her obsession with David Langermann and eagerly looked over the list I had begun the night before. I studied Amelia, trying to remember when I had been able to meet each new occurrence in life with such zest. Had my carefree days ended when I came back here to take on responsibilities?

Looking at the paintings seemed to take my attention off my personal problems, and for the next two hours I enjoyed bending over the dark canvases making out signatures and dates. After an hour or so of work, we came to a large canvas at the back of the lounge. An elderly gentleman with a bushy mustache looked out as if surveying those in the room to see if they met with his approval.

I moved closer, for I had never been able to see the painting very well while it hung in this dark corner. "I think this is my grandfather," I said. "Here, help me get it down. I can't make out the title, the plaque is so dirty."

We got the heavy painting off its hook and carried it over to the bar, where the sun reached. Then I used a rag to wipe away the layers of dust on the plaque and saw that I was right, for engraved on the copper plate in the base of the frame was the name William Meredith Lundfeld and the date, 1864.

"It *is* him," I said.

"My goodness! So that's the man who built this hotel?"

"That's right."

"He is rather stern looking, isn't he?" We had propped the painting against a pillar and both of us were tilting our heads this way and that in an effort to get the best perspective.

"He was very stern," I agreed. "It was his beliefs that caused him to prevent my mother and Gerhard Langermann from marrying."

She nodded thoughtfully.

"Yes," I said, "you can almost see it in his eyes. Certain fixed ideas that he forced on others." I sighed. "Even those he loved." Indeed, his formal pose, with one hand on his lapel and the other on the silver head of a cane, made him look as if he was going to launch into a lecture any minute.

And yet for all the grief he'd caused, I found I did not hate him. There was a brightness about the eyes, and he held his mouth rigidly as if to prevent himself from a more caring expression. I was entranced with this new find, hardly knowing what to think.

"What do you want to do with it?" Amelia asked.

I looked closely at the dirt that had adhered to the pigment. "I'd like to have it restored, then I'll hang it over the entrance in the foyer. I want Grandfather Lundfeld to see how his granddaughter will bring life back to the hotel he had such hopes for, in spite of his mistaken notions about what makes a good marriage."

Amelia gazed at me thoughtfully. "I think you have a fondness for your grandfather."

I smiled. "We'll see. Perhaps I'll find out what characteristics of his I may have inherited."

We stopped for lunch and then continued our survey of the upper floors. Maude remembered a box of tintypes she thought I might like to see, and she set about hunting for it.

Amelia and I proceeded through every room, our spirits rising with expectancy every time we fit a key into a door that had been locked these many years, for Letty and Maude had not yet opened them all. One thing puzzled me, however, when we had covered all the rooms, including the upstairs halls and the ballroom. "There are no portraits of my mother," I said to Amelia.

We had reached the bottom of the main staircase again and paused there. "Even though there are a few pictures of my father, there are none of them together and none of her alone."

Amelia puckered her brows. "Surely your grandfather would have had portraits done of his daughter just as he had that one done of himself."

"I wonder. Maude might know. And she may have found that box of tintypes by now."

We found Maude in the basement of the servants' quarters, where she had dragged a crate forward. Between the three of us, we lugged it upstairs and into the servants' dining room.

"Do you think we'll find pictures of my mother in there?" I asked.

Maude looked sadly down at the box. "Not in there. There's only the ones I had in my possession when your grandfather closed the hotel."

"Why aren't there any others? Did he not have any portraits made of her?"

"Aye, he did, and the prettiest picture she was, too, when he had her painted in a cornflower-blue dress, her golden hair all in coils on her head."

"Where is it?" I asked.

"Destroyed."

Amelia gasped and I exclaimed, "Who would do such a thing?"

She cleared her throat, frowning at me. "Your father, the captain. Enraged with grief he was that night, mad with his own loss."

"What night?"

"The night she went to meet Gerhard Langermann at the windmill. The night she was killed."

I sat down on a nearby chair, and Amelia took a seat farther along the dining table. "How did it happen?"

Maude shook her head. "When they came to tell him she'd been found dead, the captain went mad, tore around the place yelling and cursing, knocking over the vases. I was afraid he'd hurt himself and ruin the hotel, too. He spotted a small picture of her and him together, and he threw it to the floor, smashing the glass with his heel. Then he started gathering up all the pictures of her he could find. He put 'em all in a wagon in the stable yard. I tried to stop him, but I couldn't. Nobody could, and he wouldn't say where he was taking the pictures.

"When I saw him go into the lounge and grab down that beautiful painting of her your grandfather'd hung over the piano, I shook all over. I tried to pull it loose from him, but he pushed me aside, and I wasn't strong enough to fight him. He drove the wagon to the beach and started a fire. Several of the men got hold of him then, but it was too late. The pictures were burning before anyone could get the buckets of water to stop it. We was all worried that the brush would catch as well, so everyone ran to put out the fire then. The pictures were near all destroyed, though. There wasn't anything left to save. She'd gone, and her likenesses, too. As if he didn't want anything to remember her by."

I listened, shocked. Edward Barlow had done that? Was this his expression of grief, of disappointment in a wife who could not remain faithful? I looked at Amelia, who sat looking miserable, her hands clenched in her lap.

"A bonfire," I said.

"Aye, the sky was bright with flames that night."

"I can't believe it," I said.

"'Tis true. He got all of them except the ones she'd given me herself," Maude said. "The one that's in her room was mine. Later, when it was all over, I hung it there."

"He must have been very hurt," Amelia said. "After all, she did betray him, running off to her lover like that. Even though..." I knew Amelia was thinking that my mother's obsession with Gerhard was what got her killed in the end.

I shook myself. "Well, there's nothing we can do about it now. Let's open this box and finish deciding which pictures might be worth hanging."

We opened the lid and drew out a stack of tintypes, photographs and other souvenirs of the hotel from twenty years ago. There was nothing remarkable, but I took the pictures of Edward and the ones of Julie Ann to keep in my room.

In the kitchen that evening over supper, we discussed the paintings, and I asked Amelia to inquire in Greenport and find out the costs of cleaning the canvases.

After supper I walked back to the main hotel building with Amelia. "Would you like to sit up with me for a while in my room?" I asked her. We had paused at the foot of the stairs.

"If you don't mind," she said, "I'd like to finish up some work in the office."

"Oh, Amelia. You don't need to do that. Surely it can wait until morning."

She gave a small laugh. "I just want to make sure I've got the list of paintings in order. I wouldn't want to make a mistake and have the wrong ones done. If you don't mind going up alone, that is."

I hesitated to leave her by herself downstairs, but there was really no reason not to, so I left her to her self-appointed tasks.

CHAPTER EIGHT

RENOVATIONS WERE BEGUN on the dining room. The tables were removed and fixtures taken down to be polished. Johannes's army of workmen measured, plastered, scraped and hammered. He had come to my office with paint chips for me to consider, and we both bent over the worktable together as I tried to decide which of two cream colors to use for the trim. "I'm not sure, Johannes. Which do you think?"

I glanced up at him and caught a twinkle in his eye. His blond brows lifted.

"You must decide," he said gravely. "I am sure my professional opinion would be inferior to your own natural taste."

"Johannes, you are teasing me."

"I?"

His expression made me smile. I had been squinting at the colors for some time and could not tell any more which would look best.

"Perhaps Amelia can assist us," I said. "She has a good eye for color."

We were still debating the merits of the colors when Amelia rushed in, her eyes round and her cheeks flushed. With one hand she pushed her curls back from her forehead.

"He's here, in the sitting room!" she said, as I opened my mouth to inquire what had happened. "At least I asked him to wait there, but I think he's gone to have a look at the work in the dining room.''

"Who?" I asked. My pulse raced nervously as I moved toward the door, Johannes watching both of us curiously. But I knew what the answer was to my question before she even had the words out. I stepped into the lobby.

She followed me. "David Langermann. He asked to see you."

I saw him picking his way through the construction rubble in his black morning coat and gray serge trousers, and I moistened my lips and pressed my hands to my hair. He turned, and we faced each other across the length of the lobby and the lounge.

I could not imagine what he wanted, after what he had said to me. Behind me I heard a commotion and babble of voices. I turned to see Maude, who had come through the lobby. She stopped in her tracks as David came toward us.

"I am sorry if I've come at an inconvenient time," he said. "I could have sent word, but I thought it just as efficient to come myself."

My face warmed. "Forgive the mess. We are in the midst of construction."

"I can see that."

Amelia was standing by Maude, her eyes wide. I cast a glance at David and saw him looking attentively at the young woman.

"Amelia, this is David Langermann," I said. "David, Amelia Tucker, my assistant." He stepped forward and bowed over the hand she gave him.

"I'm pleased to meet you, Mr. Langermann." She blushed, and I could see that she was entranced by him. I felt oddly annoyed at his charming manner.

When I introduced Maude to David, she bobbed her head, saying nothing. I then extended the introductions to include Johannes, who had just entered the lobby. The two men bowed formally to each other, but did not shake hands, acknowledging the difference in their social status.

"What brings you to Orient Point?" I asked David when the greetings were finished.

"I have business to discuss with you privately," he answered.

"Of course. I think we will be comfortable in here," I said, indicating the sitting room, which was clean if not refurbished.

As the others exited, I asked Maude to send us some tea. She bobbed a clumsy curtsy and disappeared. I pressed my lips together. She'd never curtsied to me. Indeed, I noticed that David Langermann's presence was creating some interesting effects on my household staff. Amelia retired to our office, and I had no doubt she would do her best to eavesdrop if our voices carried that far.

I walked to the far end of the room and stood before the brick fireplace. As David glanced around, taking in the details, I was aware of the same turbulent emotions that I had felt when I saw him last.

"Why have you come?" I asked. My words sounded sharper than I had meant them to.

"You left my house rather abruptly, and I wanted to apologize for your discomfort, which I am sure was caused by my indiscretion."

"Oh?"

"The music box," he said.

I jerked my chin up. "Yes."

Maude brought in the tea things and set them on a low table in front of the sofa. I sat down and poured. My hands shook, but I preferred to have something to do with them.

"Is that why you've come?" I said presently. "To apologize?"

He set his cup on a side table. "No." He reached into his breast pocket and withdrew a leather wallet. From that he extracted a piece of paper and handed it to me.

I stared at it for a moment, then raised my eyes to him. "What does this mean?"

"It is a bank draft for the amount you indicated you needed."

"I did not expect it."

"I realize that."

"That is, you expressed, er, doubts about the venture."

He stood and walked slowly about the room, looking at the moldings, the carpet, the wall sconces. "So I did. But when I saw that you were determined to carry out your project, I decided it was the least I could do."

I rose. "Why?"

He stopped pacing and moved toward me. I resisted the impulse to step back. I had to stop acting as if I were afraid of him. He looked into my eyes and was so near that I could almost feel his breath on my lips. I trembled.

Then he turned back toward the fireplace. "I felt obligated."

"You mustn't feel obligated. I cannot accept this."

I held out the bank draft, but he pressed my hand back, moving close again and holding my gaze with his own. "Perhaps obligation is the wrong word. Let us say instead that I am intrigued."

"Intrigued?"

His lips curved in an ironic smile, and he said, "Enough to become a partner in the enterprise."

I started to protest again, but he gripped my hand tighter. I swallowed and said, "It is generous of you. I will try to see that your investment makes you a profit."

"You may send the necessary papers here." He gave me a card with the name and address of the attorneys who handled his affairs.

"Since you are here," I said, "perhaps you would like to see some more of the place."

"Indeed. I would like to see what my money has bought."

I choked back my misgivings, trying to be grateful for the money he had handed me, for it was much-needed financial relief. After I showed him the rest of the downstairs, we proceeded up the main staircase to the second-floor landing. I opened several of the rooms for his perusal, and then we made our way to the ballroom on the fourth floor.

My nervousness increased when we reached the double doors and I fiddled with the lock. At last I swung open the doors and we went in.

The November sunlight failed to penetrate the heavy draperies, so I crossed the room and pushed aside a pair of them to let in a broad shaft of light. David walked slowly down the room, his footsteps echoing on the polished oak floor. The only sound was of the workmen's hammers outside. Trying to dispel my trembling, I forced myself to walk toward the stage.

As if knowing what I was thinking, David said, "Does the music come from there?"

"Yes," I said, then changed course and turned away swiftly, suddenly overcome with strange feelings at being in this place with him. "If you've seen enough," I said, "we should go." I crossed the room and opened the door.

David glanced once more around the room as if memorizing its details and then followed me out.

"Will you be staying overnight?" I asked as we descended the stairs.

"Yes, perhaps for a few days—if you don't mind, that is."

I breathed deeply, and while a part of me wanted to refuse him, another could not.

"I will have a room made up for you in the west wing of the third floor," I said. "It will be away from as much of the noise as possible."

"And away from your own rooms, I'll wager."

He did nothing to lessen his cool, self-composed exterior, and I reminded myself that I must be careful around him. He paused on the second-floor landing and looked out the windows.

"I am sure my investment will be in good hands." Then he took my hand in his and brought it to his lips to kiss. I thought to pull away, but as my cold hand felt the warmth of his, I wanted him to go on holding it. I could not fight my feelings as he pulled me against him, his lips on my hair.

"David," I said, trying to move in his grasp.

"Shh," he whispered. "Do not be afraid, Erika."

My cheek melted into his shoulder, and I was shaking as he lifted my head and kissed my forehead. Then he lifted my chin with his fingers.

I saw the intense sadness in his eyes, and I was aware of the emotions that must be encompassing him, too. I had tried to convince myself that what I felt for him was compassion, but I knew that was a lie. His fingers touched my cheek, and tears rolled out from under my eyelids. *Born of the loins of sinners,* my mind hammered at me, *could we not escape the sin?*

I was lost, conscious of nothing but his strength and the blood bursting in my ears. How long we stood thus, I do not know, as he continued to kiss my forehead, my hair. My heart beat with his, and I could read his thoughts. I knew this was wrong, and my conscience fought hard to bring me back to reality before it was too late.

"Oh, David," I whispered before his mouth came down on mine. I could not stop my response, and although I knew that it was unsafe to have him in this place for even a single night, I silently prayed that he would never, never leave.

He pressed his lips once more slowly on my hair and then pushed me away, turning from me with what seemed to cost him a great deal of effort.

"I'm sorry," he said, his voice rough with emotion.

I leaned on the window frame for support, shame filling me. It was bad enough losing control of myself around him. I could not allow myself to become food for gossip, for I would be risking the success of the hotel, which would cost us all of our livelihoods. But I did not know what to do. We were blood related and yet ... so physically attracted. I was flooded with mortification.

He rested his head against his hand. I caught my breath and turned my back to the wall, my eyes closed.

"It isn't fair," he murmured. Then he straightened and ran his hand through his hair. "Forgive me."

I leaned my head toward him. "It is not all your fault, David."

He turned and rested his shoulders against the window jamb. "If not my fault, then surely my responsibility. A man is expected to control his—" he paused "—baser appetites in the presence of a lady, certainly in the presence of a lady to whom he is blood related."

His bitterness was clear, and I knew the taunting words covered his own pain. I looked away, aware of the truth. David would have to turn his attentions elsewhere. Still, I felt that the closeness between us would remain unbroken in our hearts even if we must distance ourselves physically from each other.

"Is there no woman in your life then?" I asked.

He gave a harsh laugh. "I am not insensitive to the charms of a woman." His expression made the blood throb in my throat. "Especially a lovely and admirable one."

"Admirable?"

"What am I to do, Erika? I have always taken the path of least resistance and avoided personal entanglements. Instead of confronting life, I have shut myself off from it, cloistered myself in the solid surroundings of material wealth. Now you challenge me, and I am not sure I am up to the challenge."

"What do you mean?"

"*You* intrigue me, Erika. You are not merely some shallow acquaintance I can easily dismiss. You appear out of nowhere and put forth a proposal that shakes me to the root of my being."

"I did not mean for it to be that way," I said.

"No, but it is probably good to face those things in our lives that are unpleasant. I admire your character for doing so, Erika. I find myself wishing I had your courage. Perhaps that is why I agreed to help you. To see if I could live up to it."

"Surely you exaggerate."

"I don't think so, but perhaps as I understand more myself, you, too, will better understand me."

"Perhaps."

He grimaced. "Right now my greatest challenge seems to be to keep myself from touching you."

I clenched my jaw. "We must learn to control ourselves."

"It is a pity I do not dare try to get to know my half sister better, but I would only come to care for you more than I already do."

I could see the danger in this conversation, so I turned from him and began to descend the stairs. I did not wait for David to follow, but made my way to the lobby.

Johannes was waiting there for me. "What is it?" I asked him, hoping he could not read the turmoil that must have shown on my face.

"We've found something I believe you should see. As my men were examining the north wall of the dining room, we found a passageway. Before we closed it off, I thought you should look at it."

"Of course."

Johannes glanced in the direction of the staircase, and I felt David's critical gaze follow me as I moved on with Johannes. What he showed me was truly astonishing. I peered into the opening where the wall had been broken through. Behind the supporting beams, a passageway ran the length of the dining-room wall.

"Where does it lead?"

"Follow me." He took a kerosene lamp, for it was dark inside. On our left was the solid brick wall, and on the right the frame that supported the inner wall. We passed the main staircase and came to some stairs that led sharply upward. Johannes tested them with his weight to make sure they were safe, and I followed him up. We came out on a small landing, and I held the light so he could examine the wall in front of us for an opening.

There was a panel, which Johannes was able to slide back, and I was not surprised at what lay on the other side.

My mother's bedroom. I looked around at the fluffy bed hangings and the furniture that Maude had kept polished and shook my head pitifully. So Julie Ann, with Gerhard's help, no doubt, had contrived to use the space between the inner and outer walls to construct a route to use for their rendezvous. Perhaps he had even visited her in this very room. I felt dizzy, thinking of the lengths my mother had gone to for her lover.

Had life with Edward Barlow really been so terrible that she clung to Gerhard, even after he had been driven from her? I shuddered involuntarily and tears filled my eyes. I pitied my mother her passion. Passion that had made life miserable for her, for her husband and most likely for Gerhard, too, for in the end she had driven him to kill her.

Johannes shifted his weight behind me, and I reached for my handkerchief.

"I'm sorry," I said. "I'm afraid this old place is full of surprises for us. Thank you for showing me that passageway."

Johannes's blue eyes were full of sympathy, and I tried to smile. It had been a day of emotional upheaval, but I could not allow myself to fall apart in front of this man, who, though a friend, was also an employee. I could feel his concern and warmth, but I had to show him I was strong. I walked to the door, and he followed me into the hall. At the head of the stairs, I paused.

"Please board up the passage," I told him. "We've no use for it."

"As you wish."

Downstairs I headed toward my office. I heard voices within, and came upon David and Amelia deep in discussion. I noticed how feminine Amelia looked in her frilly white blouse and gabardine skirt, and her demure glances at David were surely of the kind that encourage a man.

"I hope I'm not interrupting," I said, feeling a stab of jealousy at seeing their heads so close together.

Amelia dropped her gaze, and David shifted his weight off the table where he had been leaning. I remembered my earlier thought that he would have to turn his attentions to another woman, but now I resented the fact that he might be doing it right here under my nose.

"I'm afraid we shall have to take supper upstairs, since the workmen are in the dining room," I said. "Amelia, will you ask Maude to see that the sitting room is ready? Tell her to let me know if anything is needed."

"Yes, ma'am," said Amelia, and she slipped out.

"That is," I said to David, "unless you would prefer to have a tray sent to your room."

"Your arrangement sounds fine to me."

"Very well," I said, not looking him in the eye. "Supper will be at eight."

"Eight it is, then." He stepped forward, as if making for the door, but he stopped near me, and I could feel his gaze on my face.

"I have a few pressing matters to attend to now," I said, hating my stiff formality. But it seemed to be our only recourse, for when we spoke of things that were truly close to our hearts, we verged on dangerous territory. I watched him go, then sat down heavily. I found I was unable to concentrate on paperwork, so I sought out Maude to help her set up a temporary dining room upstairs.

Supper was an awkward affair with only David, Amelia and myself. We struggled to keep the conversation to business matters, but I felt the strain of the undercurrents.

Every time I looked at David, I caught his warm, assessing gaze. Amelia, dressed in a light blue tarlatan gown with a low square neckline, blushed at his slightest glance, and I felt both resentful and worried. She was far too young for a man of David's experience.

After supper I excused myself, along with Amelia, and retired to my room. I collapsed into my wing chair and closed my eyes. My limbs felt heavy, and I began to doze. I knew I should get up and undress and go to bed, but I was too tired to move.

Some time later I awoke to the sound of tinkling music, soft and enticing. I did not lift my eyelids though I was wide awake. I felt *her* presence, but it was not startling, and I held very still as if to move would break the spell. I felt the cool breeze come in from the window and caress my face, reminding me of the way my mother used to soothe me before I went to bed as a child. The waltz played on and on, and I found myself nodding my head to its rhythm.

"Mother, if you're here," I whispered, "tell me what you want. Tell me why you make the music play."

CHAPTER NINE

DAVID HAD BUSINESS in Patchogue and left Monday morning. I was in the dining room later that morning with Johannes and his workmen when Maude rushed in, wringing her white handkerchief in her hands.

"Maude, whatever is the matter?"

"A man's come round back. Been rescued from the sea. You'd better come."

"Can't someone just give him something to eat and send him on his way?"

"No, no, Erika. He's asking for you. He...he..." She gasped for air and I thought she was going to faint. I grasped her arm and guided her into the lounge to a chair.

"Maude. Are you all right?"

She only shook her head and gestured helplessly.

"Can I be of help?" Amelia had come in and I turned to her thankfully. "Yes, please stay with Maude, and oh, would you tell Johannes I'll be right back after I've seen what is the matter?" I hurried along the boardwalk to the main kitchen. Glancing in without entering, I saw Cook hand a man something to drink and insist he sit down in a chair by the wall.

He was of medium height with sparse gray hair. He drank from the mug, but he did not seem to want to sit in the chair until she unceremoniously pushed him.

Well, that was taken care of, I thought, and being more concerned that Maude did not faint, hurried back.

Maude was mumbling incoherently. I sent Amelia for the smelling salts, and I was still sitting with Maude when I became aware of a scuffle behind me.

Amelia had returned and was blocking the door, but the commotion had escalated, and I saw that the troublemaker was the strange man I had seen in the kitchen. Maude peered around me, and after taking one look at him began muttering invocations to the Lord.

"God in heaven, he's back from the dead," she moaned.

"Take your hands off me," said the man as one of Johannes's workmen tried to escort him out. I rose as Johannes came into the lounge. By now everyone was staring at the man while he continued to grumble. "I demand someone take me to my daughter."

I froze midstep. Maude was now moving toward him, her hands outstretched as if in a trance. The man's face was gaunt from exhaustion or undernourishment, and I finally walked forward just as he broke free of the workman's grasp.

He peered at me and I at him, my heart hammering. Then he stumbled forward and his eyes rolled up in his head as he fell. I rushed to catch him and so did Johannes. As we lowered him to the floor, his eyes fluttered open, and he said hoarsely, "Erika, is that you?"

I felt as if time were playing a trick on me. Edward Barlow was dead, lost in a shipwreck in the Auckland Islands. Who, then, could this man be?

I barely remembered my father, and the man before me looked nothing like the photographs I had seen. This had to be an impostor, perhaps someone who had known my father and had heard about me, yet in my heart a chord of recognition struck.

Johannes and his assistant looked at me inquiringly, and I struggled to regain my presence of mind. "Take him to a room upstairs," I said. "The rooms in the east wing of the second floor are clean."

Amelia fanned Maude furiously and held the smelling salts under her nose. Maude looked up as they led the man away.

"Maude," I said, "is it really him?"

"I swear it is. I ain't set eyes on him since he left here twenty years ago, but unless he's died and come back to us, I'd swear he never died at all. It is him. It is Edward Barlow."

I sent Letty to the village for the doctor, then made my way upstairs and tiptoed into the room where he had been put. He was sound asleep, so I moved closer to the bed and looked at his face. I stared at every feature, trying to decide for myself if this was the man I vaguely remembered from my childhood.

My memory of him was hazy, and there were so few photographs. I could not be sure. If it was really Edward Barlow, why had he come back now? That it coincided with the opening of the hotel gave me reason for suspicion. Perhaps this man was an impostor and was going to try to claim the hotel for himself. I crept out of the room with much to think about.

The next morning I breakfasted in my room and then went along to see what had been done for this man who claimed to be my father. When I knocked, he called out cheerfully. "Come in."

Letty had found him a change of clothing, and he was standing before the mirror above the highboy, shaving. The bowl of water in front of him was full of lather, and a towel was draped over his shoulder. He caught my eye in the mirror. "Ah, daughter, good morning to you."

I stood a little straighter. "Good morning. I've come to see if you have everything you need."

"Everything indeed and now the best thing of all, yourself."

I sat on the edge of the bed and watched him.

"Ah, I can see in your eyes, daughter, that you're not at all sure it's myself standing before you, but I can assure you, it is."

"But where have you come from? Where have you been all these years, if indeed you are my father?" I asked after a few moments, my mind swirling with doubts.

"Stranded, I was," he said, "near dead and out of my mind when they found me after that shipwreck of the Aucklands."

"You mean the *Golden Moon*?"

"Aye. Thought I was a goner, but I stayed afloat on a piece of her hull till it washed ashore."

"And you've been there ever since?"

"Till a year ago. I lived alone for many a month and finally lost my mind. That's how I was when the natives came and took me away to their own islands. Finally I was well enough to take care of myself again, and I got along, though I didn't remember who I was."

"Why didn't you try to get to the mainland, find out where you'd come from?"

"Couldn't. Aye, but it's a long story in the tellin', perhaps I'd better save it till after I've had a little breakfast."

"Yes, well, I'll have a tray sent up."

"I'd be obliged, daughter. I think I'll just rest my bones in the chair here. And if you'll join me for breakfast, I'll tell you the whole tale."

I rose. "I think the others would also like to hear it. If we could all listen at once, you wouldn't have to repeat it. Maude and Teddy would want to know."

"I'd be pleased and honored to tell my story."

"This evening, then, after you've rested, and the workmen have finished for the day."

"Tonight, then, my girl." He wiped his face with the towel and then turned to me. I was sure he could see the questions in my eyes.

I left the room and ordered him a breakfast tray. If he knew I was testing him, he did not seem to show it. I suspected he would love an audience, but more important, it would give those who had known him a chance to form their own opinions. It was still possible he was an impostor, Maude's reaction notwithstanding. She could have been fooled by his sudden appearance and his knowledge of my name.

If this was Edward Barlow, there were many implications. Most important, the hotel rightly belonged to him as long as he lived.

He spent a restful day, wandering about the grounds a little and then taking his ease in his room. My responses to him were mixed, though I held myself somewhat in check, not wanting, I supposed, to let myself think it was really my father, when it might not be so.

We assembled in the upstairs sitting room where we would not be bothered. Maude and Teddy had dispensed with their duties for the evening, and I had asked Amelia if she would like to join our group. When I told Johannes what had occurred, he insisted on staying, becoming suspicious of the man immediately; I was grateful for his protectiveness. And so we had gathered, my father taking a seat in a big armchair in front of the window, beyond which was the darkness of the sound.

"It was the twelfth of November, 1874, when we sailed out of Sydney harbor on our schooner, the *Golden Moon*. There was the master mariner, the mate and a crew of three including myself. We were bound for the South Seas on a sealing expedition. On the thirtieth of December in early evening, in dark, cloudy weather with a fresh breeze blowing, we sighted the southeast shores of the Aucklands. The sea broke on board in all directions, and a thick fog set in with drizzling rain."

He had begun to tell the tale as if he were used to holding an audience—perhaps around a tavern table? And I wondered how the story had evolved with each telling. I hoped to be able to sift through it well enough to decide if it was based on truth or not and the incredible had occurred—that Edward Barlow had come home.

Even I became entranced as he went on to describe the gale and how the ship broke up on the rocks. He'd hung on through the night, he said. Then in the morning he was thrown up on the beach and lost consciousness.

"When I came to I did not remember who or where I was. As soon as I was strong enough I went exploring and came upon a creek of clear water and an abundance of timber. I walked along the shore and saw where planking from the lifeboat lay half in the water."

He'd used the wood to make a rough hut and there spent the winter, living on fish, seals and fowl he caught with the tools he'd fashioned himself.

"At the end of what must have been July, the aurora australis shot up from the horizon—streamers of varied shades of light—and I fought the hail, rain and snow that was falling all the time then. I feared the hurricanes would blow my hut down and I would be housewrecked as well as shipwrecked."

He told how he had lost count of the number of months since he was cast away, and suffered an anguish of mind until he was wrought up into a state of frenzy. Then one day he spied what appeared to be canoes in the harbor. At first he could not believe his eyes, but when the long canoes beached, he recognized the Maori of New Zealand, fishermen who had come there for sealskins to trade with the British, who occupied their lands. They took him with them when they left, and after many days and nights at sea came to the South Island of New Zealand and took him to their village, where they lived in small rectangular huts and worked their farms. They had European clothes and farm tools as well as weapons, but he feared to cross them, for many of them adhered to their ancient cannibalistic ways. There had not been a man eaten in some time, for the people had been Christianized by the missionaries, but if slaves tried to escape or disobeyed instructions, they might still be killed.

"I learned to speak Maori and almost forgot my own language. I got a Maori wife who cared for me, and in this way I spent the next thirteen years, sometimes sailing off in the canoes to catch fish or seals. White men came through our village, but I saw no point in conversing with them now, for I was content. Besides, I had completely forgotten my other life, except for strange things that sometimes haunted my dreams.

"Then one day my life changed again. On the horizon there appeared a large sailing vessel with many sails. I was spellbound as she got nearer. I knew I'd seen such a ship before, and I found myself remembering how I had worked on the decks.

"You cannot imagine the state I was in. I feared I was losing my mind again, for I did not know what to do with such memories. I saw that the ship was making for a harbor a ways to the north, and I plunged through the thickets, coming out on the beach not far from where they anchored. In my excited state I ran forward, shouting to them and waving my arms.

"Imagine my surprise when one of them fired a shot in the air to scare me off. I took cover and watched as they lowered their boats and came ashore. They stayed for a week, and I discovered that they had among them an interpreter who understood Maori and English, which I had begun to recall myself."

Before the ship left, he'd sneaked on board and stowed away. Many days and nights he remained hidden until a yearning for fresh air and an end to his provisions drove him topside. "I could now speak sort of Pidgin English, and they took me to the captain. The ship was bound for England, and when he said 'England,' thoughts and pictures flooded my mind. I begged him to take me there. I could earn my passage for I was a sailor and could prove it.

"They thought me daft, for I gestured and threw my head about wildly. 'Put him in chains,' the captain ordered, and I protested, but they clamped me in irons on the gun deck. The longer I languished there the worse I became and I feared my old madness would return. I had hoped to make myself useful, and they had chained me up instead.

"We rounded Cape Horn in high seas, and I thought we might go down. But during that storm, it all came back to me—who I was, how I had come there, everything. Now I was going to be lost at sea again. Fate was playing a cruel trick on me.

"We made the Horn, though, and went out into the Atlantic. The captain took pity on me at last and I was released from the chains, given more food and a berth, and by the time I was recovered, we were making our way up the Thames."

Once in England, he was given clothes and a shave, then shipped onto the *Merry Weather*. The voyage was uneventful and the ship anchored in New York.

"There I met up with the crew of a three-masted schooner sailing up the East River and onto Long Island Sound. I conveniently left them at Southold. And so my friends, this is how I've come to you. It is a tale hard to believe, but true."

I looked around the circle of watchful faces. Maude was dabbing her eyes with her handkerchief. Teddy was shaking his head in stupefaction. Amelia had listened to the whole narrative wide-eyed, for it must have touched her love of adventure. Johannes had begun listening with a look of skepticism on his face, but I noticed he had nodded at several points, whether from agreement that this man who called himself my father had done the right thing or whether he thought he was telling the truth, I don't know.

For myself, I thought that even if the story had been embellished, there was truth in it. He *was* my father. I rose and went to him. "Thank you for telling us . . . Father."

I took his hands in mine. Maude and Teddy joined us and soon we were all crying.

Amelia came to wish us good-night. My father squeezed her hand warmly, then she kissed me on the cheek. "I'm so glad for you, Erika," she said.

Johannes shook my father's hand, then mine. Amelia waited by the door, and I saw her catch Johannes's eye. He hesitated, then escorted her out. Maude and Teddy said good-night, and then I stood alone with my father.

"Would you walk with me, daughter?" he said. "I've a need for some air."

"All right. I wouldn't mind a stretch myself."

We put on our coats and walked downstairs. It was late, and Maude had turned the lamps in the hallways low. When we stepped outside we found a fog had come in from the sound. I took my father's arm and we went down the path toward the boathouse.

"Ah, 'tis hard to believe I'm here," he said. "Doesn't seem like it's changed all that much. Except that you've done a good job, daughter. You've a talent for business, as I thought. That's why I left you the hotel, should anything happen to me."

"But now you're back."

"'Tis hard to believe. 'Tis hard to believe."

We had reached the wooden pier that led out to the boat house. There was no delicate way to ask my next question, so I plunged ahead. "What about your drinking, father? Do you still have a liking for liquor?"

"Only a glass now and then. Had my fill of bein' out of my head for long enough. I've no need to dull what senses I've finally got returned to me."

That was some relief. Perhaps we could get on then, I thought, if he really wanted to work. I shook my head in a sort of sad amusement at the help I had assembled here. Old Maude and Teddy, still capable in spite of their age. And there was poor old Pepys, now my father. I wondered if I, too, would grow old working at this hotel. I tried to put such discouraging thoughts aside. There was something else I had not yet mentioned to my father. David Langermann.

We had stopped on the pier by the boat house. Suddenly my father said he thought he saw movement, someone slip into the boat house, but it was too dark for him to be sure.

"Hello," I called. "Is anyone there?"

When there was no answer my father said, "Wait here, daughter. I'll go and have a look."

"No, it's too dark."

But he had already walked ahead. The fog was rolling in thicker now, and I was afraid to step too hastily for fear I would slip off the pier and into the water, which was sloshing on both sides of me.

"Father," I called out, taking careful steps along the pier. The boat house was still a few feet distant, and I could hear the lap of the water below me. I saw someone move before me and thinking it was my father, I took a few more steps that way and called out, but no one answered.

I knew I should head back, but when I turned to see how thick the fog was behind me, I could not even see the shore. I suddenly felt very alone, and very afraid. As I tried to calm myself, I heard a soft footstep, a whoosh of air behind me, and then I felt a sharp blow to my head. I staggered as pain shot through me and I struggled to hold on to consciousness. I flailed my arms madly, groping at the curling fog trying to clutch the wet boards of the pier as I fell toward the water. Then everything went black.

The next thing I was conscious of was voices coming from a great distance. I tried to move but the sharp pain shot up the back of my head. As my eyes fluttered open, the faces above me blurred.

"She's awake." It was Maude's voice.

"Now don't try to move." A man's voice.

But I was coming round rapidly. I could see them now. Dr. McCutcheon was bending over me, and Maude was sitting by my side. Edward Barlow stood at my feet, peering at me anxiously. I heard another male voice and tried to turn again, but then I winced. I thought perhaps Johannes was still here, but when the man moved into my field of vision, I saw with surprise that it was David.

"Nasty bump she'll have," said the doctor, "but nothing's broken and she's come out of it. Plenty of rest, that's what I prescribe."

"Erika, are you all right?" David replaced Maude by my side.

"David, where did you come from?"

"I returned this evening and tried to find you, but you had gone out for a walk with your..." He cleared his throat and glanced quickly behind him at Edward. "This man."

"Lucky for us all he went looking for you, too, for it was he who pulled you out of the water," said Maude.

"You," I said, trying to sit up.

Seeing that I was determined to be in a sitting position, Amelia adjusted the pillows where I lay on the daybed in my sitting room. The pain had subsided to a dull ache, and I was aware of all that was going on around me now.

"But who hit me?"

"You hit your head on the pier before you went into the water," said Maude.

"You must have lost your footing on the pier. It was damned slippery," said Teddy, who hovered beside Maude.

"No," I said. "That isn't what happened."

They all stared at me as I shook my head, albeit gingerly. "I saw Father go into the boat house. He wanted to see who else was there."

"Someone else?" said David.

"Yes. Father thought he saw someone go in there, so he went to see who it was. I called out to you, Father, but you didn't answer."

"Didn't hear you. I was on the other side of the boat house. By the time I came back I saw this here man pulling you out of the water. Gave me a scare, it did."

"Then if you hadn't come, David..." My words drifted off.

"You'd have drowned," he said flatly. I shivered.

"That still doesn't explain who hit her," said Amelia.

"No, it doesn't," said my father.

David narrowed his eyes at Edward. "Maybe he did."

"Now wait a minute—" began my father.

"Please don't argue," I begged them. "I'm sorry you have to meet like this. Father, this is David Langermann."

My father stared at David as the name registered. No one spoke, but tension crackled between the two men. David eyed my father skeptically.

Suddenly everyone began arguing about the incident by the boat house again, and I attempted to quiet them. "Please, please, you are forgetting, we were not alone. There was someone else in the boat house."

"Are you sure? Fog can play tricks on your eyes," Maude said.

"Father's sure, and I see no reason to doubt him."

"What about Pepys? He's often down there."

"It might have been Pepys," I said, "but he wouldn't strike me...."

The doctor had put his things away, and he crossed to have one last look at me. "You've got to let Erika rest now," he insisted. Maude nodded and began to shoo everyone out of the room.

When everyone was gone, Maude returned to help me undress.

"I didn't have a chance to thank David," I told her after I had pulled my nightdress over my head.

"That may be so. I just hope you're thankin' him for the right thing."

"Maude, you don't think he hit me, pushed me into the water and then pulled me out, do you? Whyever would he do that?"

"Can't say what anyone is up to around here anymore. But now you put that out of your mind and get some sleep."

I didn't argue but shut my eyes, the throbbing in my head now a dull ache, and let Maude pull the covers around me.

CHAPTER TEN

DAVID STILL HAD BUSINESS to attend to at his manufacturing plant, but concerned about my injury, he expressed his desire to stay a few days more. I couldn't say no.

Maude seemed less afraid of him, though when I came upon her unexpectedly, I could hear her whispering prayers and muttering to herself. One evening I attempted to draw her into conversation about him.

"Maude, you don't approve of David's being here, do you?"

We were in her cottage where she was sitting by the fire, squinting at a hem she was mending. "Doesn't matter what I think. He's here and he's bought into the place, and that's that."

"We did need the money, you know."

"Humph. I'm not saying David Langermann's without his charm. But it's an evil charm, it is. We'll all be better off when he leaves is all I'm sayin'."

On the day David planned to leave an invitation addressed to me arrived. I was crossing the lobby when I looked up to see David descend the staircase. I stopped in the center of the lobby, and David paused, his hand on the rail.

"I hope you're feeling better."

"Yes."

He looked as if he were about to speak again when Teddy shuffled in and handed me an envelope. I frowned at the deckle-edged paper with gold engraving. It was from a Major John Ward and the address was Shelter Island. I turned it over and opened it. Major Ward was giving a ball on the first night of December, which was three weeks away, to which my household was invited.

David crossed to where I was standing and looked at the invitation. He grunted. "I'm afraid I'll have to attend, as well."

"What do you mean?"

"I will most certainly be invited, too."

"But I don't even know the man. Why has he invited me?"

"He makes it his business to know everyone in these parts. Major Ward owns a lot of land both on the North Fork and on Shelter Island. Every year he gives an early-winter ball. He makes sure to leave out none of the large landowners from here to Southold."

"But I do not fit into the category of landowners, if you mean landlords who have enough land to lease out. All I own is this hotel and the land it stands on."

"That will suffice. If I know Major Ward, he will have heard about you." He pulled down the corners of his mouth in annoyance. "He especially makes it his business to know the wealthy young women."

"Well, I am certainly not that."

"Your position is what matters. You'll have to attend, of course. Not to do so would be a social insult."

"How can I insult him if I don't even know who he is?"

"You may not yet realize it, but society of a sort exists here. It would be unwise not to make yourself known to your neighbors. Word of mouth will do more for your business than anything else."

I shrugged. "I suppose, but I hardly have time to attend a ball." I did not like David's dictating what I must do. And I had nothing to wear, but I refrained from mentioning that.

"It would be best if you did not go unescorted," he said as if he had not heard me.

"I am not even planning to go."

"I will take you."

"You?"

He nodded. "The major was a friend of my family's, and I see him occasionally. I will tell him that it's my pleasure to escort you."

My face was flaming as I confronted him. "David, you must be mad. Surely they know who our parents were and will be aware of who we are. We cannot go together."

He raised his eyebrow at me and a muscle twitched in his cheek. "I see no better way to dispel any doubts about our relationship or to stop any rumors about the past than to appear together publicly on the best of terms."

"You can't mean it!"

"But I do. It is also customary to bring your entourage. A separate party is given for the servants. Surely you would not deny your devoted caretakers and your lovely assistant a chance to enjoy themselves at a party. And, of course, now there's your father." The last was said with some disdain, but I chose to ignore it. Instead I inhaled a deep breath and said, "I will consider the invitation."

I supposed I would have to go. I did need to become better acquainted with the locals, but I still felt uneasy about attending with David.

When he bade me goodbye before luncheon, however, he assured me he would call for our party at six o'clock the evening of the ball. We would travel from Greenport to Shelter Island in David's private launch.

After he left I let myself be persuaded that perhaps he was right. It would be a way to show the world there were no more bad feelings between our families.

Plans for the ball set the household in a flurry of activity, and I rued the fact that we three women seemed to get little else done for the next three weeks. I sent my father to the tailor in Greenport to get a proper suit.

"Oh, Erika," Amelia told me as she stood in my room for a fitting. "This will be my first real ball. You can't know how I am looking forward to it."

"Stand still, girl," muttered Maude from her seat on a low stool where she was pinning the hem. We had found a gown of my mother's that Maude was remaking for Amelia. I, on the other hand, was so much taller and longer of limb than my mother had been, that I'd had to go to the dressmaker.

Amelia would look lovely, I knew, in the midnight-blue velvet with wide white lace trim that swooped low over her bosom and shoulders. Black satin bows trimmed the flounces, and a heavy fur cape was brought out of mothballs.

When we first examined the clothes, tears had come to Maude's eyes. "I never thought these lovely things would be worn again," she had sniffled sentimentally as Amelia turned around, the skirt of the dress billowing about her.

"Well, now they will." My answer was snappish, as I was feeling out of sorts over the entire affair. My nerves were wrought up about appearing in public with David, and I was beginning to despair over the whole enterprise.

I had begun to think that perhaps there wasn't room for both David and me to run the hotel together. Perhaps he should buy me out entirely, so I could live somewhere else on the income. But then what? Without the hotel, my life would lack challenge. No. My only real chance was to open the hotel. Surely when summer came we would begin to be rewarded for our efforts. And so I let events take their course, preparing for the dreaded affair on the first night of December.

On the night of the party I donned my forest-green satin gown with pearls set in the train. Letty fussed over me while Maude attempted to dress my hair. I sat frowning in the mirror and cried out when Maude stuck my head with a hairpin.

"Quiet, child. How can I get this hair of yours to stay up unless I use pins? As it is, you've got so much hair there's hardly room for the coils on your head."

"Oh," I groaned. "Then why don't you cut some of it off?"

"Oh, no, miss!" exclaimed Letty. "Your hair is much too beautiful for that."

"Well then, do something. I can't stand all these pins sticking into me."

Maude made a larger coil, and when she was done I grudgingly appreciated their work. The hair was looped about my head, emphasizing the length of my neck, and I had tweezed my brows into a neater arch and applied enough color to my cheeks to bring out my strong cheekbones. I would do, I supposed, to meet the influential Major Ward.

Letty and Maude were dressed in their finest wool dresses, and they went ahead of me down the stairs. When I reached the stairs, I heard the front doors open, and Maude admitted David, who paused on the landing and watched me descend. His lips curved into a smile of pleasure, and I felt suddenly gratified that I had put up with Maude and Letty's ministrations.

"You do yourself proud, Erika," he said as he offered me his arm when I reached the bottom of the stairs.

"You look well also," I said. Indeed, his black cutaway with its silk facings and his snowy-white shirt with stand-up collar, which contrasted with his healthy complexion, made it difficult for me to tear my eyes away from his, which seemed content to rest on me.

We joined the others in the sitting room, and David bowed. I watched his reaction to Amelia's pretty looks, and indeed a smile lit his eyes as she blushed for him. Johannes, too, cut a handsome figure in his dark wool suit, white shirt and tie, his size and stern expression making him appear a tower of strength. I felt the tension in the air as the two men nodded to each other without smiling.

"If you are ready?" David said. Then I happened to catch Amelia's glance as David held my wrap for me. The pretty blush had disappeared from her cheeks, and instead her lips were pressed tightly together. Her eyes narrowed slightly, and as I slipped into the fur wrap I could almost feel her envy. I looked back at her, and she met my gaze with a start. Then with an almost imperceptible shrug of her shoulder, she took Johannes's arm.

Still, the realization pounded in my mind. Amelia was jealous of my relationship with David. If only she knew how innocent David's attentions must forever remain!

I pulled the fur hood close around my ears as the men donned their greatcoats, for the air outside would be sharp. David, Amelia, Johannes and I rode in David's brougham. My father, Maude, Teddy and Letty took our own buggy. In the brougham pans filled with coals helped warm our feet, and with our bulky clothes, it was a cozy fit. Johannes sat stiffly facing David, who was beside me. The carriage jerked forward and we bumped toward the road.

"Will there be many people?" I asked David to break the silence.

"Several hundred I should think, if you count everyone at both festivities."

"Major Ward must be very wealthy," Amelia said. "My father has mentioned him, but of course we were never invited to one of the balls."

The carriage swerved, and I was pressed against David's arm. His hand met my gloved one as I tried to straighten myself. My eyes flew to his, and I saw the glimmer in his pupils as his fingers closed around mine and his arm supported me. Quickly I glanced away again and concentrated on looking out the window, and I was relieved when at last we turned into Greenport and proceeded to the dock.

We left the carriage, and as we walked out onto the wharf where the steamer launch was waiting, I breathed the fresh air coming off the dark waters between Greenport and Shelter Island opposite us. David helped us on board, where we ducked into the cabin and sat on padded seats. My father stayed on deck, offering the boat's captain his expertise on getting under way.

Amelia's face was bright from the cold, and as the steam-driven motor chugged noisily, she engaged Johannes in conversation, seeming to turn all her attention from David and me.

Maude held on to the edge of her seat as if she did not feel too steady embarking on the water, even though we only had a short distance to go. "Never did take to sea travel," she said grimly.

"But Maude," Amelia protested, "this isn't the ocean. We're only in the bay."

"Same water," said Maude, and I smiled. David caught my look of amusement, and it reflected for a brief moment in his eyes. Then he looked out a porthole as if forcing himself not to share the moment of closeness with me.

We headed toward the western side of Shelter Island, where the hills rose steeply above the water, and eventually we came to a small dock jutting out from shore. A wooden staircase and railing twisted up the hill and was lost among the trees. Higher above were lights among the pines where the house was hidden. We pulled alongside, and David stood on deck as the boat's captain tossed a line to a man who waited on the dock. Behind him stood a large, powerfully built man with red hair and beard. He was dressed in a cutaway with starched white shirt.

David shouted to him. "Greetings, Major."

"David Langermann," returned the major. "I wasn't sure you'd come. I thought you might be in London by now."

We were alongside, and David stepped to the dock, taking the major's extended hand. "I soon will be, but I'd hate to miss your annual ball."

Major Ward laughed heartily and clapped David on the back.

David made introductions, and then Major Ward beamed at me, bowing over my hand and kissing it. "A pleasure, Miss Barlow," he said. Then his eyes met mine, and I saw a flash of shrewd appraisal there. He seemed to approve of what he saw, and I was oddly pleased. I took David's arm to steady myself on the dock.

"And you may remember my father, Edward Barlow," I said.

Major Ward's eyes opened wider, as my father stepped forward and put out his hand.

"It's been many a year, John, but I hope you've not forgotten an old friend. Surely you remember a few lively nights at the Swan's Down in Sag Harbor?"

Major Ward's jaw dropped, and he squinted his eyes, but as he leaned down to look closer at his "old friend," he smiled in recognition. "Why, so it is, so it is. And we'd all given you up for dead. Well, bless my soul, you're alive and in one piece. Welcome to my house, my friend." And he clapped his arm around my father, who was dwarfed beside him.

"Aye," said the major, indicating the entire party with his other arm, "you're welcome ashore. Just what my wife needs, some new company to entertain." He sent my father ahead, and then taking my arm, he walked me along the dock, pointing to the staircase. "I hope you will enjoy my little hideaway. And we've food and drink enough to keep you here for days. I have looked forward to meeting the charming new proprietress of the old hotel at Orient Point, and the daughter of my old friend."

Then he turned back to David and said, "Perhaps you gentlemen will take a glass of port with me in my study before we join the festivities."

"I've never refused the offer of a good glass yet," said Edward. I raised an eyebrow, remembering my father's comment that he took only a glass of liquor now and then.

We climbed the staircase and came out at the edge of a circular drive leading to a four-story mansion. The climb had invigorated me, making the blood throb in my temples. We made our way to the house, where a small woman stood at the pillared entrance. She directed Maude, Teddy and Letty to the servants' party in a separate hall, and Johannes and Amelia stayed with the rest of us.

"Constance," said the major to the woman, who was his wife, "you remember Edward Barlow."

His wife smiled weakly and whether or not she remembered my father I could not tell. Then the major boomed, "And this is Miss Erika Barlow."

As Constance Ward pressed my hand I saw the slightly cowed spirit in her eyes and the prim pursed lips. "You are welcome to our house," she said.

We were led into a large hall where a long table with silver candlesticks was heavily laden with roast suckling pig and other tempting dishes. Wine was poured, and for the first hour we mingled with the other guests. Constance introduced me to them all, and though I often lost sight of David, I could not help but be aware of his presence.

When the orchestra struck up the first notes, David came and bowed before me. I had noticed how the other ladies present followed him with their eyes as he crossed the room, and I felt my face flush as he turned his attentions to me, even though I remembered the purpose of our public appearance.

I felt that all the eyes in the room watched as he led me to the floor and placed his hand on my waist. But David was a graceful dancer, and I soon relaxed.

The glitter of the evening and the high spirits of the party began to make me forget my anxiety, and I was sorry to see the dance come to an end. David led me back to my seat and, bowing graciously before our hostess, led her to the floor. I saw Amelia smile engagingly at Johannes, who took her in his arms for the next dance.

I then danced with a number of gentlemen with scarcely a break. I saw my father bow before Constance Ward, and I was surprised that he was prepared to go on the dance floor after so long a time out of society, but he danced competently. Now and again I caught sight of David partnering one of the young ladies of the crowd. He danced with Amelia, too, and though I knew he must dance with every woman in the room, I could not curb my feelings of... what? Jealousy? But I knew I must. Besides, I was determined to have a good time.

Johannes finally asked me for a dance and I followed him to the dance floor. "Are you enjoying yourself, Johannes?" I asked.

"I am afraid I am not a very good dancer," he said.

"You're a fine dancer, Johannes. You mustn't underrate yourself. And I believe several of the young ladies are vying for your attention."

He frowned. "And you, Erika. You seem in high spirits."

I laughed gaily. "I must admit I had not enjoyed a dance in a very long time. I shall have to be careful not to have too much champagne."

His eyes strayed from me, and I glanced over my shoulder. David was partnering Amelia again, and she was smiling brightly at him. Johannes lifted a brow and turned me around, tightening the pressure at my waist, then finished the dance in silence. I did not think Johannes liked David, but of course he was too polite to say such a thing to me.

Then David appeared beside me. "May I have the next dance, Erika? That is, if you are not already worn out by your many partners."

"I am tired, David, but I wouldn't mind some refreshment." He nodded and followed me from the room. I accepted a plate of food and a glass of champagne, which I promised myself I would only sip, and we made our way to a table next to one of the marble pillars. The music floated to our ears from the ballroom, and I began to relax.

"Would you like to see Major Ward's collection of paintings?" David asked after we had eaten. "There is a gallery off this room."

"All right," I said. For I did not feel like dancing again.

The moon coming through the glass doors opposite illumined the gilt-framed pictures that lined the wall. "Major Ward's ancestors," David said.

"Very impressive. I see his family fought in the Revolutionary war. How did our Major Ward achieve his rank?" I asked.

"He distinguished himself in the Mexican-American war," David said. He had moved nearer me, and I could tell by his tone of voice that his mind was not on battles. I was as usual profoundly affected by his nearness, and when he took me in his arms, I did not resist.

"David," I whispered, as he brought his face near me, "why do you tempt fate?"

He smiled at my words, and his eyes drifted over my face and throat down to the rise of my breasts pressed against the velvet of his suit.

"We do tempt it, do we not?" he said, and I could hear the growing passion in his voice. "Tonight is magic, Erika. How can I take Fate seriously on such a night? With beauty all around me, and you, who are such a part of me, must we let anything mar our happiness this night?" His hand moved over the back of my dress, his fingers touching my bare skin.

"Erika, I want you. I cannot believe we are blood related. I cannot believe that what we feel for each other is wrong."

I shuddered at his touch. "I, too, wish it were not wrong," I said, for I savored the sensations I was experiencing. I had never felt their like, and I knew I never would again. Only with David, who read my mind and heart, could I share such lush unrestrained feeling, and I stifled a cry in my throat as he bent his head toward mine. I knew I should resist, but I had been too affected by the sumptuous surroundings, the sensual tastes of food and drink on my lips and tongue, and now the warmth I felt in David's arms. I knew I must never give myself to him, but neither could I stop him as he kissed me deeply.

"Erika," he moaned as he left my mouth and sought my shoulder with his lips. Were we to become lovers, then, I wondered in the fog of my mind as my body seemed to release every spring that had held me back. I had suspected I had a sensual nature, which went hand in hand with my yearning for adventure, yet it had been held in check by my upbringing. Oh, why did it have to be *this* man who threatened to free me from those imprisoning strictures!

My body was on fire, and I feared I was lost. As my mother had been lost to Gerhard Langermann so that she lay down with him on the floor of the windmill, so would I open myself to David's burning desire here in the gallery beneath the disapproving gazes of the Ward ancestors.

My sleeve had slipped farther down my arm, and David's lips were kissing my shoulder when the sound of laughter floated down the long gallery.

I gasped. "David, someone's coming."

His hands clamped over my arm and he lifted his head. I fought to regain my breath, as the voices and laughter came closer. I pulled myself up straight and turned to look at the pictures, averting my face from whoever was coming so they would not see my flushed countenance, my disarranged hair or my impassioned gaze.

David turned his back to me, walked toward the glass doors and gazed out. The group of young people had spotted us and quieted their laughter. They moved on through the gallery, and David nodded to them as they passed. The two gentlemen nodded gravely to him as the ladies hurried ahead, seeking some darkened part of the mansion, no doubt to carry on their own amorous activities.

I could not stay here any longer, and I didn't want David to go with me, fearing we would give ourselves away the minute anyone laid eyes on us.

"I believe I shall take a breath of air," I said.

"Shall I accompany you?" he asked.

I had already started for the other end of the gallery, toward the light from the other rooms. "No," I said, still feeling breathless. "I need to be alone."

He did not follow me, and I asked the butler to bring my cloak. Outside a bright moon lit the sky and reflected off the dark water far below. The forest around the house looked deep, and I headed for a small path that seemed to wind along the edge of the woods. I walked into the woods a short distance, wanting only a little solitude, but I did not plan to go far.

As my eyes grew accustomed to the darkness, I saw that the path led down the side of the hill toward a small clearing. I was about to take a step when a twig snapped behind me. I froze, then whirled about, but I could see no one.

"Hello," I called. "Is anyone there?"

No one answered, so I turned and made for the clearing, feeling safer in the open. Some sense that there was someone following me made me hasten my steps, and soon I was running along the path. I stopped at the far side of the clearing and looked back. Nothing moved, and yet I was certain I was being watched.

Panic rose in my throat as I realized I would have to go back the way I came in order to get to the house. I tried to tell myself there was nothing to fear, but the thought of plunging back into the dark woods frightened me, for from this distance, I could not even see the lights of the mansion.

I glanced to my left and saw the narrow path along the side of the hill. Then I heard again the sound of a foot stepping on leaves and a pebble rolling down the hill.

"Is anyone there?" I asked, but it came out only as a hoarse whisper. I fled down the path, sure that someone was following me now, and the fact that they did not answer me filled me with fear.

My breath came in gasps, and branches caught at my skirts, but I struggled to keep my footing on the sloping path. The route became steeper, but now I could see the wooden railing ahead. But here the path had washed out, and there was no way to get to the steps.

I glanced back, and saw a branch move where I had been. I thought of calling for help, but with the music from the party, I doubted if anyone would hear. I had no choice. I grabbed a bush that protruded from the eroded hillside and tried to jump toward a patch of ground that looked as if it would support me. My fear gave me the strength to take the leap, and as I flung myself across the ground, I thought I heard laughter behind me—an eerie, horrible sound, almost inhuman.

I struggled in the bushes where I landed. Tears blinded my vision. My dress was torn, my hands scratched. But I crawled toward the steps, still some distance away. The soil was loose, and I began to slide, crying out as my handholds gave way.

I was tumbling now, rolling over in the dirt. When I hit the bottom, the breath was knocked out of me. Then I heard footsteps in the gravel and feared it was my assailant. Suddenly, miraculously, David was by my side.

"Erika, my God, what's happened? I came outside, and I thought I heard your voice."

I blinked at him, unable to speak as he felt my limbs to see if anything was broken. "Can you move?" he said.

"I think so," I whispered.

He got one arm under my knees, the other holding my trembling back and shoulders.

"Oh, thank God you're here, David," I murmured. "Someone followed me."

"Shh, don't try to talk," he said, as he lifted me. He carried me to the pier and then set me on my feet as he untied the ropes that moored his launch.

I started shaking now that the terror and the danger were past. David assisted me into the boat, then settled me in the cabin before he started the engine. I did not know where the boat's captain had gone, but he had probably joined the servants' party, not expecting to leave so soon.

As I wiped tears and sweat on my torn sleeve, I asked, "What will they say when they find we've gone?"

"The others can swim."

A smile forced its way to my swollen lips. How like him, I was discovering—decisive, stubborn, yet able to make a joke. Still, I *was* concerned about the others, and I wondered how they'd get home. David assured me that the major would see to their transportation, and I had to be satisfied with that.

When we had made some distance, he idled the motor and came to examine me. "You have a scratch here," David said, pulling back my hair and examining a small cut on my brow. "I'll dress it."

I protested, but he wouldn't listen to me and rummaged in a medicine cabinet for a salve and a small bandage. I let him minister to me, the throbbing in my head gradually lessening. The picture of someone following me flashed before my eyes. I could not understand why someone would want to frighten me. I tried to tell David what had happened, but my words were incoherent.

"If I find out who was trying to frighten you," David said, "I'll kill him."

"David, don't say that."

His angry look became mixed with doubt, fear and passion.

"Let's get you home," he said.

A wave of emotion swept over me, and I removed my arms from the blankets and reached for him. He came to me, holding my trembling body in his iron grip. My tears welled up again, and I clung to him as he kissed me tenderly, caressing me gently until I was calm.

Finally he laid my head on the blanket and pushed himself away from me so he could drive the boat. I closed my eyes, aware that we were moving, and then I let myself fall asleep, peacefully enshrouded in the cocoon of David's care.

CHAPTER ELEVEN

THE NEXT MORNING I rose well before the others, who had got home very late. Wanting only a chance to order my thoughts, I left the hotel and went for a walk. My boots crunched along the gravel-strewn path that led along the narrow peninsula across the road, and the wind from the water buffeted against me in spite of my hooded ulster. I walked for some time toward the point and finally seated myself on the sand, watching the turbulent waters of the bay. The events of the night before pressed in on me.

Tears of frustration came to my eyes. A few months ago when I had thrown myself into the project of renovating the hotel, I had been full of hope. Now I wondered if I should continue. Reluctantly I returned to the path and began my slow walk to the main road and the hotel. As I looked ahead I saw a figure on the path coming toward me. It was David.

"You've been gone some time," he said when we were within speaking distance. "I told Maude I would look for you."

"Yes," I said. We gazed at each other, but there seemed little else to say.

"I am leaving. I've come to say goodbye."

I blinked my eyes against the sudden moisture there.

"Yes," was all I said. His departure was what I wanted. Why then was there a sudden dullness in my heart as I imagined the cold, damp winter months as I plodded through my work, probably never to lay eyes on David again. And after the concern he had shown last night, I realized I had begun to depend on him in subtle ways. But no matter how I felt, our relationship could not be.

"I do not intend to leave you here alone," he said. "Someone tried to frighten you last night, Erika, and we do not know who."

"Then you believe there was really someone there."

"Of course."

I did not say it, but there were some who might suggest that David himself was the one who had frightened me, perhaps the one who had hit me on the head weeks before.

"I plan to leave my groom, Charles. He has served as my bodyguard on a number of occasions, and he can be trusted."

"Do you really think it's necessary?"

"I'm afraid I do."

He had turned and began walking with me slowly, as if neither of us was in a hurry to meet the main road. Here with the wild elements of the peninsula it was easier to walk side by side, each knowing the other's thoughts. When we were alone together, I could almost imagine that there was no one else. It was when we were thrust out into the world in which we lived that we could not look at each other.

"I'll be going abroad soon," he said.

"To spend the winter holidaying in London."

"Damn!" he swore, swinging around suddenly and gripping my shoulders. "There will be no joy for me in it," he went on. "In past seasons I have thrown myself into an oblivion of social activities, drinking and indulging in pleasures of the senses. It took me away from here, from my past. In Europe I am only an eligible bachelor with money to spend. But then I had vowed never to marry, only allowing myself to take pleasure where I found it, where I did not have to know the name of the woman who shared my bed."

I averted my gaze, his words stinging me. "Can this season not be so for you as well?" I asked. "Can you not leave this part of the world behind you? Forget me, David." The tears were slipping down my nose, freezing on my skin. My hood slipped back, and his chin brushed my hair.

"No, Erika, it cannot be so. I thought my heart was locked against feelings of the kind you have aroused in me. I fought it, but you have won."

"I have won?"

He tipped my head up to look into my eyes. "I love you, Erika."

"As a brother loves a sister?"

I saw the pain sear across his eyes, but it was no worse than the pain in my heart. No matter how cruel it sounded, I had to force David to accept the truth of our situation as I had to accept it myself.

The blow had its effect. He turned his face away and exhaled. "You know that is not the way I feel about you."

He had dropped his arms, but we still stood very close. "It is no use, David. We cannot go on fooling ourselves. Perhaps it is some sort of trial put to us by a cruel Fate. Perhaps we must face this trial in order to be rid of the curse forever."

"The sins of the father?" he said bitterly.

"I don't know, David. But we could never be truly happy the way other people can be happy."

He reached for me again. "No one would know, Erika. We would be far away. It would be only you and I."

I shook my head, swallowing the bitter taste in my throat. "We would know, and our children."

His eyes narrowed, and the emotion I saw there tore at my heart. I was crying silently, but I had to say these hated words once and for all.

"And everyone else would know eventually. They would see it in our faces. We would be outcasts. You might be accepted in your fashionable European circles, but what would I have, David? Nothing. For a woman's reputation is her only means of acceptance by others. If you leave me here, I will be unhappy, but I will have a . . . a life."

His face was contorted with bitterness, and I saw the struggle in his eyes. I knew in that instant how much he did love me, for I saw the sacrifice he was going to make. He took my hand slowly and raised it to his lips. Then he turned and walked away.

I followed slowly, just in time to see him open the door to his carriage, which was waiting in the drive. No one else was about except his driver, who was hauling the reins up to the seat, and Charles, the groom.

David said a few words to Charles, who glanced in my direction, nodded and then took himself off to the stables. I supposed I could tell Teddy I had hired him to look after the horses. A bodyguard. The thought made me shiver.

David ducked into the carriage. The driver slapped the reins, and the carriage pulled away.

I don't know how long I stood there. My lips were frozen and frost had gathered in my hair, the hood still thrown back on the shoulders. I stared at the empty road that wound around the stark trees where the carriage had disappeared.

I felt a presence at my elbow, and then Maude said, "Won't you come in, child? Cook's made some hot soup."

I followed her numbly. Once inside the kitchen I took off the long-sleeved ulster with great effort and stood by the fire thawing my limbs. After eating, I left the others and went upstairs. I did not stop at my room, however, but climbed to the top floor. I fumbled in my pocket for the heavy key to the ballroom and opened the doors. An air of sadness filled the dilapidated room, which still awaited the craftsmen to restore it to its former glitter.

I walked across the floor in a stupor, grief pulling at my heart, wishing suddenly I'd never come to Orient Point, wishing I had never learned about my mother's lover or met David Langermann.

I flung open the doors to the terrace and greeted the cold gust of air that burst in. Then I sank to the floor, clinging to the heavy draperies. A cry rose in my throat, and I sobbed into the woven material, muffling my wails, as my shoulders shook violently, and I spent my grief. I was in love with David. I sobbed loud and long, and later I wondered that no one heard me. If they did, perhaps they thought it was the ghost mourning her lost lover.

My sobs shortened, and soon I lay on the material of the drapes that I had brought down with me. My tears had stained everything, but I felt some relief from the outpouring of grief. I lay there uncaring what would happen to me next.

I might have fallen asleep except that my limbs soon felt the hardness of the floor, adding bruises to my inner pain. I sat up and took in a breath of freezing air. I did not know how, but I would have to go on. I forced myself to get up, and closed the doors against the winter cold. I left the ballroom, went to my room and made a fire, sitting before it thinking.

I could close the place, send David's money back, dismiss the servants. But aside from my own living to think about, what right had I to cast all my employees upon the world where they would have to begin again?

Or, I could live a decent life here if I could bear the loss I felt in my heart now. And if I could find out why someone or something was threatening me, for I could ignore that fact no longer.

I sent word that I did not want any dinner. Letty came and tried to make me at least have some tea. When I undressed for bed, I sat at my dressing table, and my eye fell on the small packet of my mother's letters. These letters had given me my first clue about David and his father, Gerhard. With a sudden decision, I took the packet into the sitting room where a few flames still reached up from the glowing coals.

"Too long have I dwelled on the past," I whispered to myself. I held the letters over the flame until a corner caught and I watched as the blackness ate its way across the stiff paper toward my fingers. Then I threw the packet in. The fire leaped up, and I half expected to hear my mother's haunting music and sobbing as if in protest, but I heard nothing.

As the ashes blew up the chimney, I thought I sensed a lifting of a burden from my shoulders. At least something of the past was gone now, and I was determined to get on with my own life.

I DO NOT KNOW HOW I managed to get through the next weeks. I believe Maude and the others knew something of my state for they were very solicitous of me. I forced myself to go through the motions of living, even to the point of letting Amelia help me write advertisements for the hotel and place them in various newspapers in New York and Connecticut to attract visitors for the coming summer.

My father spent more time along the docks in Greenport, even going out with the fishing fleets. He also drank more often. Sometimes when I watched him weave back to the hotel and up to his room, I would stand at the bottom of the stairs, my fists clenched, filled with a foreboding of what his drinking might cause....

Johannes was supervising interior work now and consulted with me frequently. Once we were sitting together in the sitting room where we had discussed business and had been reluctant to end the afternoon. Instead we turned our conversation toward our homes, and I spoke to him of the people I had grown up with in Maine.

"Autumn there is beautiful," I said. "The colors are so vibrant and the air can be so still that, it is as if you have left the rest of the world behind."

"Do you not find it so here?"

"In the winter, yes. It has been very quiet." I sipped my tea. "I have needed to be quiet. And you, Johannes, have you lived all your life in Southold?"

"Most of it. My family have always been fishermen here."

"But not you?"

He smiled. "I wanted to work with my hands. I wanted to feel the wood, use it to fill men's needs."

I smiled back at him and watched the fire reflect in his eyes. I felt my fondness for Johannes grow. He was so comfortable to be with.

I rose and walked to the fireplace, stretching out my fingers to warm them. Johannes rose and followed me. For a while we stood side by side, looking into the yellow-orange glow that reflected on our faces. Finally, he spoke.

"You do not mind my company, then?" he said.

"Of course not, Johannes. I enjoy it."

I looked at his broad face, his bushy blond mustache, his caring eyes. "You are a good man, a good friend."

"I see unhappiness in your eyes," he said, his voice full of warmth. "I know where your thoughts lie. But your lover does not come for you. Why?"

I flashed him a look. "He is not my lover."

"A woman would lie about such a thing to save her honor. She would not want her reputation tainted."

"That is true, and I will admit that at one time I might have lost my virtue—" I shut my eyes "—to David."

His jaw clenched. "What right does such a man have to dally with a woman of virtue?"

My lips trembled, but I felt I owed him an explanation. "You must not think ill of David. His motives are misunderstood."

"I understand that a man toys with a woman's feelings, leading her into danger where he is not prepared for the consequences."

"No, Johannes, it is not like that. David has feelings for me, only—" I hesitated "—we cannot ever consummate them." I had not meant to say this much, but I could not let David take all the blame. Nor could I lie to Johannes, for I felt that I needed his friendship. "Surely you know about..."

"Yes. I have heard stories about your families. That is why I cannot understand how you could be attracted to the son of your mother's murderer."

"He is not—" I stopped myself and sighed. "I cannot explain, Johannes. You must simply try to understand me. I'm sorry, I can say no more." I shook my head. "You are kind, Johannes. I consider you my friend, but..." I gestured helplessly.

He gave me a look of sympathy and reached out to place a hand comfortingly on my shoulder. We were still standing this way when Amelia entered the room. She stopped short, her eyes flying from one to the other of us.

We separated and I said, "What is it, Amelia?"

"I wondered if you wanted to go over the china inventory now." She glanced at Johannes, and I thought I saw resentment spark in her eyes. "But I can leave it for you in the office."

"That would be fine." I smiled easily, my spirits lifted after my talk with Johannes. She left, and then I saw him to the door.

As he said goodbye, he took my hand. "I am worried about you, Erika," he said. "Perhaps it is not my business, but I have a feeling this place is not safe for you."

My skin prickled. "What do you mean?"

He moved his head almost imperceptibly. "I know nothing, but there was the accident the night your father returned."

"Yes," I said.

"And there was the mishap at Shelter Island."

I had never told anyone about the incident the night of Major Ward's ball—only that I had slipped and torn my dress and so David had brought me home early. "If someone wants to hurt me, they have certainly not made it apparent why."

I felt the slight pressure of his hands. "In any case, with winter coming on, my men and I have accepted your offer of living quarters. I will feel better if you have more protection."

"Thank you, Johannes, but I hate to cause you worry."

He tried to give me a smile as I opened the door. "I will decide about that," he said.

I closed the door behind him. It had felt comforting to spend a few hours with him, and I wondered not for the first time if he were beginning to think of me as more than a friend.

I went to the office to find Amelia tidying up a stack of papers. "Shall we go over the list of china now?" I said. My tone was more lighthearted than it had been for some months, and by contrast Amelia's voice sounded strangely flat.

"If you wish."

We went over the list, itemizing what pieces needed replacing, what sets needed completing so that we could serve a hundred guests. Amelia kept her eyes glued to the papers in front of her and displayed none of her usual gregariousness.

Presently I asked, "Amelia, is there anything wrong?"

"No," she said, but she did not look at me.

"Nothing wrong, and yet your mouth is drawn down and you've nothing to chatter about. It is not like you."

She shrugged. "If I may say so, Erika, you are not one to criticize, seeing as how you allow yourself whatever mood suits you."

I studied her. Her lips were pushed forward into a pout, and her eyes lacked luster. Then I remembered her look of resentment and surprise when she'd found Johannes and me standing next to each other by the fireplace.

"Amelia, are you jealous of my friendship with Johannes?"

She jerked her chin forward. "How would you know what I think of Johannes? What does it matter, anyway?"

"Amelia, do stop pouting. Johannes and I are only friends. I told him so myself."

"Why are you telling me this?"

"So you know that I do not have the sort of feelings for him that a woman should have who might marry him."

"Like you have for David Langermann." Then she bit her lip. Still the dark look in her eyes told me she did not regret what she had said even if it hurt me.

I gave her a level look. "You cannot understand my feelings for David. In any case, I will not be seeing him again."

She frowned. "I don't understand. I thought..." She looked down, unable to continue.

Was it so transparent then? I sighed. "In any case, Amelia, if you like Johannes, perhaps you should let him know it. He would make a girl such as you a fine husband."

"He is kind to me, but what am I beside you, Erika?"

"My dear girl, there is nothing about me that you need compare yourself with. You are young and pretty and bright. It is all you need to be."

"But you are so sophisticated and beautiful."

I widened my eyes in surprise. "What makes you say that?"

"Erika, you really can't see yourself, can you? I've seen the way men watch you, the way you walk with your head held so high, with your golden hair and your determination. Men admire you."

I saw that she meant what she said, but there was something else there, too, that seemed to stop her from giving the compliment freely. There was still a seed of jealousy, but I could see no reason for her to feel that way.

I smiled. "Thank you for the compliments." Then I added more seriously, "But my dear, you have many good qualities yourself, and they will increase with maturity."

"They will?"

I winked at her. "I can assure you, from my own experience." I thought perhaps to tease her out of her serious mood. I had so wanted a real friendship with Amelia. I wanted to make her see that she'd no need to be jealous of me, that people admired her for herself. If Amelia was interested in Johannes, it would give me more reason to discourage any interest he might develop in me. And I felt that her father would approve of the tall Norwegian.

It was settled, I decided as I squeezed Amelia's hand and coaxed a smile out of her. I would encourage Johannes to look in her direction.

I also buried thoughts of David. Since I had not heard from him, I assumed he had succeeded in taking up his social life in Europe and had forgotten me also. Perhaps one day when we were older and less subject to unruly passions we could think fondly of each other and I could prove myself worthy of his financial investment. I hoped to return him a profit from the hotel so that he would at least not have to regret our business transaction.

As the winter months rolled in, the sounds of scraping and hammering filled the premises. The workmen were not able to work outdoors now, but most of the structural repairs were finished, and by March, the interiors would be papered and painted.

Things were progressing well, and I began to feel highly optimistic of success. I had no foreshadowing of what was to come.

CHAPTER TWELVE

It was late February. One night I had slept for some hours when I was awakened by shouts. I tossed in my bed, thinking they were part of my dreams. Then I smelled it. Smoke. I struggled up from the depths of my dreams as someone beat on my door. Panic filled me. I threw the covers aside and grabbed my dressing gown while stepping into a pair of slippers, then made by way to the sitting room, which was already smoke-filled.

Fear gripped me as I saw the tongues of flame that licked under my door. I ran back to pull a blanket off the bed and then returned, but as I reached the door handle, I jerked back my hand from the heated metal. Tears stung my eyes. I was trapped.

From a great distance it seemed, I heard a man's voice calling my name.

"Help!" I screamed. "Help." Then I heard a heavy thud on the other side of the door, and the voice called, "Stand back!"

I moved away from the door as it crashed inward, and Johannes appeared, his face smudged with smoke. He took the blanket from my hands, threw it around me and picked me up. Then he plunged back through the flames that seemed to be enveloping the room. He set me down in the hall and we ran for the staircase.

The smoke was so thick I could barely see, but there were more voices on the stairs, and when we reached the bottom I could see that everyone on the premises had been roused, and they were sending up buckets of water. Charles, David's groom, bounded toward me.

"I'm all right, Charles," I said in a low voice.

He nodded and left to help Johannes's men, who raced up the stairs with bags of sand and more blankets.

Maude, in her nightdress, threw her arms around me. "Praise be, I was afraid you were trapped," she said, clasping me to her breast.

"Amelia!" I exclaimed, then headed back toward the stairs, but Maude held me back. "She's outside. She was downstairs when it started."

Johannes, in shirtsleeves and suspendered trousers, directed the men who were working frantically to prevent the fire from spreading.

"Come," I said to Maude. "We've got to help."

I stopped Teddy, who was lugging a bucket of water into the lobby. "I'll do that," I shouted. "Take the buggy to Orient Inn and ask them for help. Then see if there's anyone at the ferry terminal. Tell them to bring blankets and pails. Hurry." We didn't have time for the volunteer fire brigade to arrive from Orient if we were to keep the fire from spreading.

Teddy hurried to the stable, and I ran to the well. Amelia looked at me wide-eyed as I took the bucket she had just filled and handed her another.

"Erika, thank goodness! I was afraid you were asleep in there. As soon as I saw the flames I went for Johannes to get you out."

We worked feverishly as more people poured into the yard to help. I stared up at the crackling flames that filled two windows on the second floor, and my heart pounded frantically as I threw myself into fighting the fire. After what seemed hours, we began to get it under control.

The men tromped through the smoke-filled upstairs putting out every last spark. Their faces were smudged with black as was everyone's who had been near the blaze. Finally, Johannes appeared and stood before me as I scooped a drink of water from a bucket we had just drawn from the well.

"It's out now, Erika. Would you like to inspect the damage?"

"Oh, thank you, Johannes. I don't know what we would have done if you and your men hadn't been here." I trudged after him inside. Smoke still lingered on the stairs although every door and window had been opened, and what I saw inside appalled me.

"Oh, no." I moaned as I stepped over the lumps of sand on the floor and made my way into the blackened rooms, still holding onto Johannes's sleeve.

"The fire must have started in here," he said, pointing to the room next to mine—Amelia's room.

I stepped toward what used to be the door. Nothing was left untouched. The four-poster was a black skeleton, and the hangings and rugs were charred threads.

"Why?" I whispered to myself, horrified at the damage. The fire had spread from her room into the hall, and the wallpaper had blistered while the fire had eaten into the woodwork and two other rooms. I felt weak as I realized how narrowly I had escaped.

"The fireplace," Johannes was saying. "She must have left the screen off while she was downstairs. A log could have fallen out onto the rug. The supporting beams are still standing, and it's only this floor. The sandbags on the stairs kept it from spreading."

His professional eye was surveying the room, and I was glad he was there, for I would not have known where to begin assessing such damage.

My head was throbbing, and I turned from the scene, wanting another drink of water and the chance to bathe my face and arms. Johannes followed me downstairs and Maude brought me a clean wet cloth.

"Do you know how it got started?" she asked, wiping her own face with her apron.

"The fireplace in Amelia's room was left unattended, it seems, and a log rolled out."

Maude pinched her mouth together as she squinted at me. "And where was she?"

"Downstairs," I said. I didn't like what I was thinking. I knew Amelia still had some jealous feelings about me, but I simply could not believe she had started the fire on purpose.

Hadn't Amelia worked through the night with the others restoring what order they could? Hadn't she squeezed my hand in relief when she saw that I was safe? Still, in the depths of her eyes there was something I could not recognize. A flicker of guilt, perhaps, that she had been downstairs when I was caught in the flames? I could not be certain.

The hotel was far too smoky to sleep in, so Amelia and I took hastily prepared rooms in the servants' quarters. We made our way across to the building while Maude went to see about linens for our beds.

"Do you think we can salvage the second floor?" she asked.

"It will be a big job, but I'm determined to repair the damage. I owe it—" I paused "—to myself."

She looked at me, her tired eyes sunken in hollow sockets.

"I'm going to dispel the . . . the evil that inhabits this place, if it's the last thing I do," I said, turning back to study the blackened windows of the second floor.

We stood for a moment, and then she yawned. "I'll see you in the morning."

"Thank you for your help, Amelia."

Maude brought me one of her clean nightdresses, and I threw off my ruined gown. After sponging myself off from the basin on the small pine table, I put on the clean nightdress and fell into bed. I was still disturbed about the way the fire might have started, but I was far too tired to think about it.

Getting up late the next day, I found that Letty had dragged some clothes that had not been ruined from my room. Most of my wardrobe had either been singed or smoke-damaged as the flames had licked across the armoire and burned my trunk, but a few garments were still usable. I put on a practical muslin dress of red and brown checks with red flannel petticoat and went across to the hotel and up to the second floor where Johannes already had workmen cleaning up. The scars from the fire and the skeletons of furniture looked even worse in the harsh light of the crisp winter day, and a feeling of depression descended about me.

Seeing me standing on the stairs, Johannes crossed to speak to me. I noticed that his hair and beard had been singed, and I shivered thinking how near to the flames he had come rescuing me last night.

"Good morning, Johannes. I see your men are already hard at work. Have you been able to assess the damage?"

"From what I can see, we'll need to replace this wing and part of another. I will have estimates to you by midday."

"Thank you." I sighed heavily. "Come to my office when you are ready with the estimates then."

He nodded and left me. I felt slightly nauseated as I looked at the destruction and imagined what it would cost to repair it, but no matter what, I was determined to go ahead with my plans. I wondered, though, how seriously this would put Johannes's men behind schedule, for I could not afford to delay opening past June the first, when the tourists arrived for summer vacations.

Amelia came into the office. "Good morning," I said.

"Erika," she said in a somber tone. "It looks awful." She looked at traces of soot she had picked up on her fingers. "It makes me feel just terrible."

"I daresay it will be a job cleaning it up."

She nodded, her eyes averted, and we proceeded to the kitchen for some breakfast. After last night's interrupted sleep, I needed a strong cup of coffee to raise my spirits. I felt ill at ease with Amelia, not knowing how to put the questions that had formed in my mind. After we ate, we helped Cook tidy up the kitchen, which was a shambles after being ransacked the night before for buckets and pails that would hold water.

Having done our share in the kitchen during the morning, Amelia and I repaired to the office. In the afternoon Johannes brought his estimates of the damage as promised, and when I looked them over, my heart sank, though I tried to keep a calm expression.

I looked up at him. "They seem fair estimates. You may go ahead and order the necessary lumber."

He nodded. "As you wish," he said. "If I put extra men on, we can still finish by the end of May."

I nodded. "All right. Do whatever is necessary."

The next day I climbed the stairs to the third floor. I had my mind on other matters, and so I looked up with a start to see my father on the landing above me.

"Oh, Father, I didn't see you." I walked up the last few steps to stand beside him, but he was staring past me.

"Father, are you all right?"

Slowly he turned his head toward me, but his eyes did not seem to focus. "Aye, there's evil here. *Her* evil. She's never left this place."

I could see that he wasn't himself, and his words made me extremely nervous. "Father, what are you talking about?"

"Your mother, damn her, her spirit won't let us rest! Surely you can tell it's her that's caused this fire."

He reached out to grab my arms, catching me off balance. "Your mother," he ranted. "It's her!"

"You must get hold of yourself, Father," I said, struggling to find my voice. "The fire started in Amelia's room. She left the screen off and sparks caught on the upholstery."

"Ha," he grunted, and for a moment we swayed there on the top step. Finally, he looked over my face, as if making sure who I was. Then he let loose my arms and half turned from me.

"I'm thinkin' of signin' on to one of the ships in the docks in New York harbor. I'm too young to retire, daughter. Might as well wrap these hands around a steerin' wheel and navigate a ship through the sea-lanes again. Can't end my days dried up on the beach like I'd be if I stayed here."

"If that's what you want, Father," I said, my voice shaking. "When will you go?"

"This time tomorrow, daughter."

I bit my lip, feeling awkward. He made no move to embrace me. I felt we hadn't had a chance to get to know each other, and so I had not developed my feelings for him to the extent that I could express any real affection. There were times like now when he seemed to be a total stranger. Still, I took his hand in mine.

"You'll come back, won't you, Father?"

I thought his gnarled features softened for an instant, and then he squared his shoulders and raised his face as if to the distant shores he was determined to see again.

"Best not to make promises. Maybe I'll come back for your summer do."

I gave him a half smile. I knew he referred to the grand-opening ball I intended to have.

"Very well then." It saddened me that I had found Edward Barlow only to lose him again, but he was right. Already I had begun to worry about the ill effects this place might have had on him. It would be good for him to sail away again, seek new horizons. But I would always remember the relationship we shared, however peculiar, and the fact that he had given me his name.

CHAPTER THIRTEEN

THOUGH THE MARCH RAINS kept us indoors, I began to feel better about the inroads we were making on the repairs to the hotel. I moved back into my room on the second floor, now completely rebuilt after the fire.

I noticed that Amelia found many opportunities to engage Johannes in discussion. When I saw them looking over plans together, I thought surely he must notice her quick mind and feminine qualities. At those times I would slip away with only a pang of regret in my heart, with every passing month feeling more and more like the spinster I was likely to become. Still, I had my work, and I was determined to put on a good face.

I came out of my office one day to find Amelia and Johannes standing at the bottom of the main staircase, their heads close together. When they heard me, they glanced up and Amelia's eyes widened as if she were afraid I'd overheard them. When she looked at me like that, I felt uneasy, wondering if she were hiding something.

We'd had no more discussions about the fire, and I had pushed from my mind the ugly thoughts that she might have caused it. Amelia might not like me as much as I'd hoped, but surely she would never actually try to kill me. As to her scheming to attract a husband, that was natural, and as long as I showed her she had no reason to be jealous of me, surely all would be well.

I decided it was time to have Johannes sand and stain the rolltop desk. I had used it during the winter but had not got to every crack and crevice.

Amelia and I emptied the contents, stacking the papers and ledgers on the worktable. I pulled the two front drawers out, then crawled under the desk and peered at the back where the drawers had fitted. Something seemed to be stuck in the corner. I saw now why the shutter did not go all the way back. A small leather volume was in the way.

"What is it?" asked Amelia, who was crouched beside me.

"I'm not sure," I said, tugging at the volume with both hands. "It's a leather-bound book of some sort."

"Why on earth would anyone want to put it in there?"

"I don't know."

"Unless," said Amelia, now on her hands and knees, "they meant to hide it."

I gave a final jerk and the volume fell out into my hands. Flecks of paper that had broken off from the pages fell onto the floor. I could see that the binding was old.

"I've got it," I said as I backed out on my hands and knees, bringing the volume with me.

"Let me see," said Amelia as she made room for me to stand up.

It was a journal. The ink had faded, and as we peered at the slanted handwriting, I saw that the entries were dated 1863. I turned to the first page, but I did not need to see the signature on the bottom to know it was my mother's.

"Julie Ann Lundfeld Barlow," Amelia read aloud.

I sat down and turned the old pages carefully. The entries continued through 1863 and into 1864, the year I was born. The last entry was from May, ending with: "How I long to see him again. Perhaps I have only imagined that he still loves me, still desires me. Such joy in my heart when I received his letter today. For when we last parted, I did not think that he would answer my letters."

My face flushed as I realized that in this diary I would find, perhaps, revealing statements about my mother's love affair with Gerhard Langermann. The letters I had read had given me some idea, but many of them had been written before she married Edward Barlow, and the later letters, mostly outpourings of emotion and reminiscences, had contained few details of what actually occurred between the two lovers. A diary meant for no one's eyes but its owner's would tell me more. I closed the volume and pressed it against my breast.

Amelia, realizing the personal nature of the book, had ceased to read over my shoulder. "How exciting for you," she said. "Are you going to read it?"

"Yes, of course. This is quite a surprise." I put it aside on the table with the ledgers. "After we finish here."

Her eyes strayed to the diary, but we completed our task, and then I sent her to tell Johannes I had cleared out the desk. I took the diary upstairs, telling Letty on the way that I wanted no interruptions until suppertime.

I opened my windows wide, letting in the fresh cool air, and settled myself in my wing chair to read. The very same chair, I thought ironically, in which I had destroyed my mother's letters only two months ago, and

I wondered momentarily if I should do the same with the diary.

I had closed a door on my mother's past and had succeeded in getting on with my life. If I read the diary, I would be opening that door again. My hand hesitated on the volume, but my curiosity was too great. Already I remembered what I had read downstairs, something about my mother thinking she would not see Gerhard again. This was the first I knew that they had thought of ending their affair.

I opened the volume. I had to know.

I had to squint at the faded ink, but soon I grew used to my mother's hand, and the words began to flow. My pulse pounded as I realized I was trespassing on my mother's private thoughts. Still, her words lured me on.

Many of the entries echoed her letters, recalling pledges of love the two had made when they were sixteen. There on the pebbly beach, they would hold hands and sun themselves on a summer's day.

But that was well before Julie Ann's marriage, a mere dream to clutch in her moments of sheer desperation at the misery her life had become. Her husband hated her. She knew now he'd only married her because her father had promised him a secure income from the hotel. But Edward Barlow could not stay sober long enough to do a day's work, much less command the respect it took to entertain guests and manage a staff.

I continued to scan the writing page by page. While reading the letters I'd had to read between the lines, but here in the diary, nothing was held back. I couldn't help but feel sorry for a woman whose bitterness had lasted so many years. Of course, it had been unfair of my grandfather to prevent Gerhard and Julie Ann from marrying. I supposed I should feel sorry for her, but instead I found that I had developed a sort of impatience with it all. Didn't I, too, know what it was to want a man with all my heart and yet not be able to have him?

I turned more pages. She mentioned Edward, but always disparagingly. He drank. His advances were distasteful. Then she would launch into tearful reminiscences about how she and Gerhard used to meet.

I read avidly, the heat in my own body rising as I read the intimate details. After they decided to marry, she recalled, their ardor had only increased, and they would meet at their secret place, sometimes at night with only the moonlight and the water and rocks surrounding them. There they would lie down on the beach, and he would caress her.

And then had come the terrible day Julie Ann told her father that she and Gerhard were planning to marry. He had flown into a rage and absolutely forbade such a union. His daughter would not marry a man outside her own church. He ordered her never to see Gerhard again.

Julie Ann was distraught. If her father forbade her to marry the man she loved, then she would run away with him. She begged Gerhard to take her away, but alas, he had no money to do so. His father was ill, and he had to take care of their farm.

Finally, even though there was to be no wedding, they consummated their love. What joy she felt giving herself to him! This was no sin, to love physically as an expression of a bond between their hearts.

As she recalled their passionate affair in the pages of the diary, she rued the passing of the years since those early days. Time had made a lie of their declarations of love. Her father had forced her to marry another, and seeing no way for them to be together, Gerhard had succumbed to William Lundfeld's tyranny and moved to the South Fork to start anew. There he took a wife, Lydia Schecter.

I was nearly at the end of the volume, and I read on anxiously. Julie Ann had prayed to be strong like Gerhard, whose marriage had kept him away from her, but she could not help her weakness and she begged to see him again.

I read the next passage twice and then stared straight ahead at nothing. I focused on the words, making sure I understood them, for what the diary said next, I could not believe was true. I stood up, shaking. Then I closed the volume and ran into the hall. I had to find Maude and show her the passage that changed everything.

CHAPTER FOURTEEN

MAUDE WAS in the laundry room in back of the servants' quarters. The building was set into a slope, and I plummeted down the path, catching myself on the turn at the bottom. I opened the screen door, breathing so hard I could hardly speak. Maude was cranking the handle on the wringer, sending the clothes through the rubber rollers that flattened them stiffly.

"Land sakes, child, what's wrong?"

I was gasping for breath, but I managed to hold out the diary to her. "It's my mother's," I said. Maude finished putting a blouse through the wringer and dried her hands on her apron. Then she removed her spectacles from her pocket and put them on.

She looked at the volume curiously as I said, "It's a volume from her diary. I found it in the rolltop desk where it was hidden. Look." I held it open so she could see the writing.

She squinted at it, then shook her head. "I never could make out her handwriting. You read it out loud to me if there's something you're wantin' me to know."

I nodded, pulling her over to the wooden bench in front of the windows. I picked up the diary and turned to the pages near the end. My voice shook as I read: "'Gerhard has not come to me since his marriage. Only I bear bitter witness to the fact that he has been faithful to the woman he married. No one will know the hurt he dealt me that magical night when he came to love me one last time and told me we could never meet again. How I clung to him and wept. I swore I would not let him go, but he left me then forever.

"'My husband believes I am Gerhard's mistress still. I don't care what Edward thinks so I've let him go on believing that. Edward was drunk the night he got me with child, and he does not remember it. And so, let everyone say the child I carry is Gerhard's. How I wish it were so, for then it would be a child of our love. Edward has only used my body for his conjugal rights, planting his seed in me when I did not want it. Let him think me unfaithful. No one will believe the words of a tainted woman whose only sin was to love.'

"Maude," I said. "Can it be true? Am I Edward Barlow's child after all? Is she telling the truth, or is this some fabrication of an hysterical mind?"

Maude frowned first at the diary and then at me. "It might be true." Then she shook her head. "They were lovers, that I know for sure. But Gerhard married and I never saw him again. I don't know. She carried on so, I thought surely they still found a way to meet."

She pressed her lips shut, heaving her shoulders heavily. "When you came, Edward acknowledged you as his own. He'd been to sea, but he returned for the birth. I heard their fights, poor thing. I know he hit her once, left her bruised."

"Didn't she tell him the truth?"

"Who's to say now that they're all gone? Maybe she wanted to spite him, poor creature."

I sighed in frustration. "It seems all they did was take out their bitterness on each other. How could they have tolerated such a marriage?" I closed my eyes and leaned on the window frame, the weight of the ugliness and blame descending upon me as if I had been there to see it all myself.

"My father," I murmured. Of course my birth certificate said I was his child. It was only later, as I grew up and found my mother's letters, that I had come to the conclusion that I was a bastard child.

"It is too much to believe," I whispered. I shut my eyes as dizziness threatened to overtake me. Then in rude shock, I opened them again. "David," I whispered, rising. "I must see him." For David could not be my half brother if what the diary said was true. I started toward the door, saying his name, but Maude called to me.

"Child," she said, "wait. You cannot go to him now. You are in too much of a state."

I pressed her arms. I was still trembling, but I knew what I must do. I left her and climbed the hill to the stables, where I found Teddy. I knew Maude would not approve of my going, but I could not stay to try to persuade her. My heart was beating wildly. I did not even know what I would say to David when I saw him. I only knew that I must see him and show him what my mother had written.

"Teddy, I will need the buggy early tomorrow morning. I must go out." Not taking time to explain fully to anyone, I hurried back into the hotel.

I went to the office where Amelia whirled around, her eyes on me. "What is it?" she asked.

"Can you get along without me for a few days?" I asked. "I must go to the South Fork."

Her eyes widened, and she came to me. "Something's happened. What is it? Oh, Erika, do tell me. What is it?"

"I..." I hesitated. David must be the next person to know, and besides, I couldn't be absolutely sure that it was really true that he and I were not related. When we met, he, too, had believed we were. No, I had to see him, sort it out. "I must see David," was all I said.

"The diary," Amelia said. "You've found something in the diary, haven't you?"

I gave a small nod and turned away, fearing she would guess the truth.

The next morning when I said goodbye to Maude, she grumbled and wrung her hands.

"I don't like it," she said as I bent to kiss her cheek. Teddy was already putting my traveling case into the buggy. I decided against taking Letty with me this time. It was fair weather, and I knew the way, and the girl was needed here.

"Don't worry, Maude. Everything will be all right. I must show him the diary, that is all. We must clear the air of the lie we have been living with."

She shook her head. "There's evil things at work here, I'm sure of it. If you go, something terrible will happen. Lord 'a mercy." She turned her eyes heavenward and I didn't argue with her except to try to reassure her against worrying about my safety.

She watched me climb into the buggy, and in spite of the nervous beating of my heart I gave her a bright smile. She only clasped her hands in front of her and watched the buggy pull away. My intention was to drive as quickly as I could without straining my horses. It was still early, and I was hopeful that I could complete the journey to Mulgrove House by nightfall.

I was impatient to see David, and yet also thankful that I had some time to prepare myself. I knew I had been victim of some of the same feelings that had made my mother throw herself at Gerhard Langermann until he could no longer tolerate the threats that must have surrounded their illicit love.

Perhaps Gerhard had grown tired of Julie Ann and turned his attentions to his wife. Whether that or he was simply doing his duty, I would never know. Nor would I know why he met my mother at the Hook Windmill the night he strangled her. But something had brought them together one last time. What? Even as one mystery was solved, another thrust itself forward, demanding an answer.

I had not long to wait in Greenport for the ferry. On the ride across the bay I stood on deck, letting the wind blow in my face as the water rushed by below. I made the drive across Shelter Island without incident, and by the time I had crossed on the second ferry to the South Fork I was quite hungry. I stopped at the hotel at Sag Harbor and ate a hearty repast.

Soon I was on my way again, and it was late afternoon by the time I drove through East Hampton village and set my face toward Mulgrove House. I was again famished when I pulled into the drive. When Mrs. Hanson opened the door, I tried to still my rise of excitement.

"Good evening, Mrs. Hanson," I said. "I am sorry to arrive unannounced, but I have urgent business with Mr. Langermann. Is he in?"

"Come in," said the German housekeeper. "Have you traveled all the way here today? You surely need some refreshments." She hustled me into the large parlor and sent Otto to have the groom attend my horses. Then she said, "Mr. Langermann is not here. I hope you have not come all this way for nothing."

"Where is he? May I wait?"

"Waiting will do you no good this time, for he is still in England."

"England!"

"*Ja.* He has not returned from wintering there. I don't know when he will be back, for he has not sent any word."

"Oh," I said, sitting down. "I knew he'd gone abroad, but I hadn't thought he would stay this long."

"You must spend the night here in any case. Mr. Langermann would want it. Now, will you have some tea?"

Mrs. Hanson left, and I stood and paced about the room. How could I have been so stupid? I had been so anxious to get to Mulgrove House with the diary that I had not stopped to consider whether or not he would be here. I pressed my hands to my face, glad there was no one else present at the moment to observe my embarrassment.

Mrs. Hanson returned with tea. "I'll show you to your room when you're ready. Would you be wanting supper sent up on a tray?"

"Yes, that would be fine."

When I finished my tea, she led me upstairs to the same room I had slept in before. When Otto brought up my luggage, I changed into a fresh gown for dinner, even though I would be dining alone.

Feeling confined, I went down to the library and poured myself a glass of sherry. I sipped at it and wandered about in front of the bookshelves. None of the titles stamped in gold on the leather bindings tempted me this time, for my mind was whirling in other directions. I sat down at the desk and ran my hand over the smooth veneer. Then I opened a drawer and located a piece of stationery, which I drew out and placed on the blotter. I tested the inkwell for ink. I knew what I would do.

I would leave the diary for David to read. Perhaps it was better that way. He could draw his own conclusions. At least I would spare both of us the embarrassment of his having to read the personal account of my mother's feelings in my presence.

Yes, it was better this way. I scribbled a brief note informing him that I had found the volume, that it might be of interest to him. I called his attention to the pages on which my mother revealed her desire to let others believe I was Gerhard's daughter. I slipped out of the library and made my way to David's study. There, I placed the volume in the only drawer that was unlocked. Then I folded my note, placed it in an envelope and tucked it in the corner of the blotter where he would find it as soon as he sat down there.

I went to bed feeling I had done what I could. It was difficult not to feel impatient, but I tried not to speculate, attempting instead to distract myself with thoughts of work. By the time I fell asleep I was imagining our grand opening, with visitors arriving from New York. I knew that for the next two months I might be able to keep my mind fully occupied.

CHAPTER FIFTEEN

THE HOTEL TOOK ON new elegance in the weeks that followed, and I turned my mind from thoughts of when David might be coming home to the work I still had before me. I found much pleasure in contemplating the placement of each picture we hung on freshly painted or papered walls. With every spot of dirt removed from the building's facade, I felt I erased some of its past.

With June fast approaching, my duties began to change. I visited the dressmaker in Greenport to acquire gowns in which to greet guests and be the hostess at evening affairs. Amelia and I interviewed hundreds of applicants for positions as waiters and maids while still consulting with the artisans who were cleaning the gasoliers and applying gilt to the mirror frames in the ballroom. The work was exhilarating, and I found I had something to look forward to every day.

At last came the night of the grand-opening ball. How excited I felt when Amelia and Teddy helped me hang the banner over our entranceway to announce the grand opening. Tonight the refurbished ballroom would glitter and sparkle with its new flocked wallpaper of burgundy and gold. The gasoliers would shine on elegantly clad couples just as I had always dreamed.

As he'd said, my father did return from New York in time for the event. He had even hired himself a valet, who was dressing him in the fine new clothes he had bought in New York—and undoubtedly charged to me. I planned to speak to him about the diary as soon as we had time alone together.

I was examining myself in the mirror in my new turquoise gown of watered silk, when Maude knocked and entered, dressed in a high-necked black silk dress with white lace collar and cuffs.

"Mercy girl, look at you!"

I turned around and said gaily, "Do you think I'll do as hostess? You don't think it's too daring a dress for the proprietress?" The off-the-shoulder sleeves exposed a wide expanse of skin, and I noticed when I curtsied before the glass that the turquoise tulle bodice gave a rather generous view of my bosom. And I would have to be careful so as not to entangle my feet in my train of corded silk. I was turning this way and that when I realized Maude was squinting at me and wringing her handkerchief.

"What's the matter?" I asked. "I know I have to be careful about the neckline, but—"

"It isn't that." She gave a little jerk of the head. "Miss Erika, he's downstairs waiting for you. Says he's come to escort you to the ball."

"Who's downstairs?"

"Mr. Langermann. He's in the lounge."

I nearly stumbled as I turned around to face her. "David? Here?"

"Yes, I'm afraid so. Now sit down, my dear. Don't excite yourself. Damned young pup, surprising us like that. He could have sent word."

"Did he say why he didn't?"

"He only just returned from abroad, it seems."

"Yes, of course." I patted my cheeks with my hands. "Well, then I'll go down and see him." I took a breath and drew on my elbow-length gloves.

Maude held the door for me and I walked slowly along the hall, the watered silk and foulard petticoats rustling about me. I paused with my hand on the newel post as I reached the stairs. The voices from the lobby rose up to me. Then, with my gloved hand on the balustrade I made my way carefully down. I turned on the landing and descended the last flight, now plushly carpeted in deep red.

I had reached the next to the last step when I paused. David disengaged himself from the group he had been talking to and looked across at me. My heart contracted as I met his glance. He looked elegant in a black tailcoat and a white waistcoat, shirt and tie. His hair seemed thicker, his face tanned, and his eyes brilliant and clear.

As he gazed at me an expression of satisfaction filled his eyes and he lifted his lips in a smile, causing me to turn a deep shade of crimson, and I was glad to have the balustrade for support.

He walked forward slowly until he was directly beneath me. The din had quieted and I felt several pairs of eyes on us as he bowed deeply before me and then raised his hand to enclose my own trembling one. Without taking my eyes from his face, I descended the last steps to the floor and stood in front of him.

"You look beautiful, Erika, and may I congratulate you on what you've done here." He gestured at the new opulence of the lobby.

I smiled with nervous pride. "It is rather hard to believe we've put it through so much change." I moistened my lips, which were very dry. "I did not know you would be here."

"I would not have missed it."

He held his arm for me to take and then led me to the lounge where the waiters were serving champagne. I spotted Johannes standing with Amelia, who looked very lovely in a cherry-colored faille gown with matching flowers in her hair. She glanced once at David and me and then turned all her charms on Johannes, smiling brilliantly at him.

David signaled for a waiter and then handed me a glass from the tray. Our eyes met over the rim of the crystal and I felt a tingle run down my spine. I felt jubilant, dizzy with happiness at his being here. Still, I held my tongue, aware that whatever we said would be heard by everyone around us, many of whom we now nodded to and greeted. His gaze lingered on my face as he sipped from his glass, then his gaze trailed down my figure, pausing long enough to admire the décolleté of my gown, where my bosom rose and fell with excitement.

"You are exceedingly lovely, Erika," he whispered, and then replacing his glass on a tray, he turned to greet the other guests.

Satin gowns, black cutaways, creamy white shoulders and the clink of glasses formed an ambience of charm and elegance, and I was thankful that my only responsibility at the moment was to smile and mingle with my guests, accepting their good wishes.

I was in midsentence with the owner of the Orient Point Inn when I overheard David telling another gentleman that his ship had come into New York port only two nights ago. He had stayed last night in Patchogue.

"Then you haven't seen your home in half a year?" the gentleman said.

"That is so. I stopped at my business yesterday and then took the steamer here."

I lost the train of thought of my own conversation, but it didn't seem to matter. I was aware that David had turned back to me. Luckily I had said nothing of a personal nature to him. Since he had not been to Mulgrove House, he did not yet know of my discovery of the diary. And it would be difficult, I feared, to find an opportunity to discuss the matter this evening, as it was such a public occasion. I hastily finished my conversation with the owner of the Orient Point Inn and moved on to the next guest.

When it was time, we proceeded up the stairs to the ballroom, where the doors were thrown open and the orchestra leader lifted his baton. David led me to the center of the room, and then with a slight lift of the eyebrow, he took me in his arms and swept me across the floor. We moved as one, and I became caught up in the beauty of the music, and the swirling movements of the dance.

Still, I was keenly aware of his hand on my waist, of the admiring glances of the other dancers and of David's relaxed expression. How I wished I might speak to him alone, and yet a part of me did not want to do anything that might detract from the momentousness of the occasion. For I had dreamed of such a glamorous ball ever since I was a little girl of four—to be dancing among ladies and gentlemen dressed and bejeweled like kings and queens.

"I am living out a dream," I said when I had breath enough to speak.

"And I," he said when the music stopped.

Then we were partnered by others for some time. I saw David dance with Amelia and wondered how he would find her loveliness and growing maturity after his six-month absence.

Finally, during the second hour of dancing, he came to me again and took my hand. The orchestra leader raised his baton and began a waltz. My eyes widened as we took the first step. It was the waltz that had haunted this room, the tune David's music box also played. A feeling of uneasiness overcame me, and as I looked into David's dark eyes, his look hardened, and his face became a mask.

I felt suddenly frightened. I was not sure of what, but I could not tear my gaze from David's face even though I had a desire to flee the room. I felt disoriented and disconnected from my body as if I were looking down on the scene. And I was not sure I was watching Erika and David, or Gerhard and Julie Ann. I became even more confused and dizzy as we continued to circle the room.

Then we were moving toward the French doors open to the balcony. We stopped dancing, and as I strove to keep my balance, David steered me through the doors. The breeze touched my hair and I walked to the stone railing, willing my feelings of disorientation to stop.

"The music," I whispered, but David was near me, turning me in his arms, his face hovering near mine as I looked into his face. I had not recovered from the disturbance the waltz had caused in me, and the intensity of David's expression only heightened it.

When he touched his cheek to my temple and held me in a guarded embrace, I could feel the tenseness in his muscles, almost as if he were afraid of his own responses.

"David," I whispered, my cheek still pressed against his shoulder. His heart beat rapidly against mine.

"I tried to forget you, Erika. My desire for you has kept me on another continent, far away."

He broke away from me and walked to the railing, looking out at the dark waters of the sound. Clouds passed over the half moon, and I could hear the water washing over the beach in a demanding rhythm. I stepped toward him, reaching for his sleeve. "It is not as you think, David. I have found something you must see."

At first I did not think he had heard me. Then he turned his head and seemed to focus on me more clearly. "My mother's diary. I came upon it when we took everything out of her desk. It was hidden in the back."

"A diary?"

"Yes. It reveals much, David. My mother writes of what happened between herself and your father."

He looked into the darkness, and I was afraid I had lost him again. "David, listen to me. She spoke of how she did not see him after he married your mother. He would not go to her after that, even though she begged him to. She must have been the one obsessed, not he. David, do you understand what I am telling you? My father could not have been Gerhard Langermann."

At last my words had some effect. He turned and stared at me as if I were the one who was mad. Then his brows came down, and he took my arm roughly. "Are you sure? Is this not some fabrication to cover up their liaison?"

"I am sure of nothing. I only read what she wrote in the diary. I took it to Mulgrove House and left it for you with a letter. You must read it, David, and see for yourself.''

He continued to hold his gaze on me, the impact of my words sinking in. "I find this hard to believe."

"Yes, I can understand that. I, too, did not know what to believe at first. Our parents loved each other, that is true, David, but perhaps your father was morally stronger. Perhaps—'' I lowered my head and shrugged ''—he grew tired of her after she had become another man's wife.'' I felt the shame creep over me as I said it.

"You and I," I finally said, "are not . . .''

"Blood related?" When I looked up his face had the curious expression I had so often seen on him. It was as if he hid his real thoughts behind a mask of irony, amused at the sad antics of the world, bitter and yet laughing at the misery.

"There you have it," I said. I trembled slightly as the breeze played over my skin. David inhaled and turned around, leaning on the balcony with both hands.

"Will you read my mother's diary?" I went on.

He nodded, but his eyes were veiled like one used to disappointment, unwilling to trust any hopeful evidence. "Perhaps it is only someone's idea of a very tasteless joke. Perhaps someone wanted us to believe what is not true, to tempt us further into our own obsession.''

"Who would do such a thing?"

He did not answer me, but pulled me to him. He kissed me once more on the lips, and I felt the old urgency spring between us.

"Erika," he murmured again, raising his head. "It is too much to hope for.'' His dark eyes held deep passion, and I knew that whatever restraints he had put on himself before were now likely to burst if he no longer believed me his own flesh and blood.

I, too, yearned for him, but I knew it was reckless to be doing what we were doing at this moment, with the ball and guests in such close proximity. Apparently David realized the same thing for he set me some distance away from him, reaching out a hand to replace a wayward strand of my hair. We took some moments to regain our composure and then he said in a low voice, "Let us wait then until I see what this diary has to say."

When we reentered the ballroom, a gentleman approached David and engaged him in conversation. I stood at the edge of the floor, adjusting my eyes to the glittering light. Amelia and Johannes, who were standing across the room together, saw me come in. Amelia walked over to me.

"Are you all right, Erika? You look flushed." I thought the expression on her face held disappointment.

"I'm fine. I told David—" But I stopped, remembering that Amelia did not know my secret.

"Come with me to have some refreshment," said Amelia. "Then you must tell me."

She led me to the end of the room where waiters in brocaded vests were serving punch. I reached for a glass, and when Amelia had hers we took seats in the corner of the room. The music and conversation served to shield us so that I was certain no one was listening. I don't know why I succumbed to confiding in her, but her interest egged me on.

"Is it something about the diary?" she asked after taking a swallow of the fruity liquid.

"Yes. It told me something I do not know whether or not to believe."

"About Gerhard Langermann?"

"Well, yes. You see when I first knew my mother had had a—" I lifted my head "—lover..." Amelia's eyebrow lifted, but I went on. "It was Gerhard Langermann, David's father, and I thought that we, that is, David and I..."

Her eyes were widened with the excitement and her lips parted slightly as she listened.

"I thought we must be blood related, because everyone at the time said I was the child of the—" I cleared my throat "—illicit union. And David thought so, too." My cheeks were burning, and I wondered at the wisdom of bringing all this up now. But I had started and I knew I had to finish.

"You are in love with him," she said.

"I don't know, Amelia. I had—" I gestured helplessly "—feelings for him."

"I thought as much."

"But I could allow nothing to happen. It would have been very wrong for the two of us...." I did not finish, but she nodded in understanding.

I hurried on. "But it may not be so now. My mother's diary said that she and Gerhard Langermann stopped seeing each other after he married Lydia Schecter."

Amelia blinked. "But they were lovers before that."

"Yes. There were certain passages that confirmed that. But you see," I continued, "if they did not meet after his marriage, which was only a few months after hers, then my father must have been Edward Barlow— for I was born much later."

"How can you be sure they didn't meet?"

"I can't be, Amelia. But why would my mother write in her diary that she did not meet her lover even though she admitted wanting to. She would have presumed no one else would read it.''

"Perhaps." Amelia's eyes narrowed. "Unless she wanted to save her reputation in the eyes of her daughter.''

I looked at her. "But how could she know I would ever find the diary?''

She leaned forward, her words coming breathlessly. "Did she not know that one day you would inherit the hotel? Could she not have planned to leave the diary for you?''

"But the diary was hidden. How could she expect me to find it?''

"She had planned to leave it for you, perhaps to read when you grew up. But she didn't have a chance to dig it out of hiding, to make a will, you see. He murdered her first.''

I sat rigidly. "No," I said. "I can't believe my mother would write lies in her diary to save her reputation.''

"She *could* have. You can't *know*.''

"Amelia." Johannes had come up on my left. How much of our conversation he had heard I did not know, but from the flushed look of his face, I gathered he had overheard something of what we said.

Amelia looked up at him suddenly, and I at her, my stomach muscles clenched with the tension her words had created. I rose and moved as quickly as I could through the doors and down the stairs, running along the hall until I reached my rooms. I closed the door behind me and went to my bedroom where I flung the windows open and breathed deeply.

Amelia. She was still infatuated with David. She wanted me to believe I couldn't have him. If David and I were related, it would leave him free for her to pursue. I had been wrong when I thought she had turned her attentions from him to Johannes. She had not. She had only suppressed her plans until he returned from Europe.

I shook my head. This was not the same Amelia I had hired, the sensible girl I thought would grow into a responsible woman. I closed my eyes and let the cool air wash over my face. What did she want of me? David? The hotel? Then I turned away, glad for the solitude of my rooms. Above me the orchestra played on, reminding me of the ghostly music that had drifted down to me when there was no orchestra to play it.

I sat down on my bed and held my face in my hands. Had Amelia deliberately started the fire? Had she tried to drown me at the boat house before that? I drew a deep breath and divested myself of my clothes in preparation for bed. I still did not know what David would do, but regardless of what happened between us I had many things to sort out first. I turned down the lamps and went to bed long before the music above me stopped.

CHAPTER SIXTEEN

THE FOLLOWING MORNING, my father came to see me while I was at the little writing desk in my room trying to organize my thoughts.

"Are you feeling better, daughter?" he asked, after I bade him enter. "I believe you went to bed early last night."

"Yes, I did." I eyed him curiously. "Father," I said. "I have something to ask you."

He rubbed his beard and stepped farther into the room. "What might that be?"

I took a deep breath and said, "It's about your disappearing all those years ago. After mother..." I had difficulty saying it. "After she died."

"I wanted to put as much distance between myself and this place as possible." He closed his eyes. "It's only bitter memories I have of this place, Erika."

"I know. I'm sorry, Father. It must have been hard for you." I was careful to gauge his reaction to my next question. "Did you love her?"

He clasped his hands behind him. "I made her a good husband. Not that I was perfect. I don't pretend it. But the woman lived in her dreamworld, she did. She was flighty, and I tried to tame her, but she wouldn't listen to me."

"But she learned to run the hotel, didn't she? You weren't much help to her, after all, were you, what with your drinking."

He gave me a gruff look that made me uncomfortable. "Drink was the only company I had. I tried to make her obey me, but she was stubborn."

"You can't force a person to love."

He shook his head, looking at his hands. "I gave up on her and went to sea again."

"Leaving her to see her lover."

He raised his eyes to me and I saw how his pupils had dilated. His nostrils flared slightly as he said, "She never stopped seein' him."

My throat tightened. It was not what I wanted to hear. "Did she not stop seeing him? After he moved to the South Fork?"

He tightened his hands into fists. "How am I to know what she did? I'd seen her runnin' off to meet him after our wedding day. I beat her for that, I'm not ashamed to say, and she deserved it. But she wouldn't settle down. I sailed away leavin' her to her precious lover, if that's what she wanted. Your mother was a harlot, she was."

"Meaning she was a romantic young girl with runaway passions. Can you not admit it, Father? It must have been that beauty and passionate nature that attracted you to her yourself."

He stepped forward and his look frightened me. "Well, I didn't expect her to be flauntin' her looks after we was married, and not to that spineless lover of hers." His eyes were dark with the rage he felt. I had risen and backed up against the fireplace.

"I found my mother's diary in the rolltop desk downstairs."

He stared at me, an eerie light coming into his eyes.

"I read it, Father, and I don't think she was lying when she wrote in her very own diary."

"Lyin' about what?"

"Before I tell you, I want to ask you a question, and I want an honest answer. There were rumors that you were away when I was conceived. Even though you came back and claimed me as your own, I grew up thinking I was not really your child."

He gathered his brows in a knot. "I know what folks thought. Oh, I came ashore and demanded my conjugal rights. I wasn't away the whole time. She may not've liked it, but I wasn't gonna pay no whore when I had my own woman. She wasn't gonna deny me that."

Tears welled up in me even though his way of speaking was coarse and offensive. "Then you did really conceive me."

He waved a hand. "How do I know whose you were? When I accused her of sleepin' with her lover, she wouldn't deny it. She must've been guilty, otherwise she would've told me different."

"Father, you must read the diary and then tell me what you think."

"Can't see that it matters much. Can't trust the words of a woman. Lies is all they are." My father turned and I exhaled, realizing how tense I'd been. "Now you must tell me something, daughter."

"Yes?"

"What is David Langermann to you?"

"I love him."

He walked back to me and gripped my chin in his hand, forcing me to look at him. His expression darkened again as he said, "Just as I feared. He's cursed you like his father cursed your mother."

"Why do you say such things? Just because of the same prejudices my grandfather had against the Langermanns? You've no right to interfere."

He clenched his fists and for an instant I was afraid he would hit me. "Not my own daughter. I'll not have it. That man will not get his hands on this property!"

I was shocked by his outburst. "Surely you do not believe that is what David wants?"

"He wants my daughter, and he wants the land his daddy would have owned had he married Julie Ann. It's revenge he wants and he'll not get it."

"Father, it is I who sought out David. I wanted to know him. I thought we were blood related, you see...." My cheeks were still warm and the words rushed out. "I suppose I was curious. Later, I knew it was wrong of me."

"You're cursed," he growled. "Cursed with your mother's sinful nature. I would have disciplined you, kept you from your mother's evil ways."

His eyes were glazed, and I'd lost hope of reasoning with him, but still I stubbornly persisted. "Would you marry me to the man of your choice the way Grandfather Lundfeld did? And have me live a life of misery and frustration like my mother's?" My feelings had escaped my control and I crossed to the door, opening it for him. "Thank you Father, for telling me what I needed to know. I believe I am capable of my own decisions now."

"You've your mother's bad blood. It's what I was afraid of." Then he left the room and disappeared down the hall.

It took me some time to regain control of my emotions, but I had work to do. I descended to the lobby where Amelia was busy adding up the breakfast tabs.

She looked up quickly in acknowledgement of my presence, though she seemed to be having difficulty meeting my gaze. I knew I would have to speak to her. I had been shocked and hurt by her words last night, and worried that there might actually be more to her behavior than I knew. I would have to deal with her somehow, but I prayed that my suspicions were unfounded, and that she did not really mean me any harm.

"Amelia," I said, "if you've finished with the breakfast receipts, I'd like to go over the reservations for next month."

"Yes, all right," she said. "I'll bring them in."

I settled myself in the office at the newly refinished rolltop desk and looked over the copies of our advertisements appearing in New York and Connecticut papers.

"Here are the reservations," Amelia said, handing them to me.

"Thank you. Amelia," I said, feeling it was the right time to speak. "Last night—"

But she stopped me with a look. "I know. You're going to say I lost my head when I said all those things about your mother. I don't know why I said them."

"I believe I know why."

"Why?"

"Because you hope that David and I *are* actually half brother and sister."

She shrugged, not looking at me. "Why should I care about that? I was just thinking what your mother might do if she were guilty and wanted to save her reputation. I know I was just speculating." She lifted her chin. "I say things without thinking sometimes."

"Amelia, you must tell me honestly. What are your feelings for David Langermann?"

She was silent.

"Isn't it true that you are attracted to him, and that is the reason you don't want it to be possible for David and I to be together?"

"What's wrong with setting my sights on someone wealthy and handsome?"

"There's nothing wrong with it, Amelia. It's just that David may be a difficult man. He's not really happy, you see."

"Because his father was a murderer?"

"Perhaps."

"Well, I don't care. He's got to marry someday."

"I'm not so sure."

"Why not? He can't just live alone forever. Who will he leave his land to?" She pressed her lips together, and I decided to leave the matter for the moment.

"We'll just have to let things work themselves out," I said. "You can't force such matters."

If Amelia was going to be stubborn about it, she would end up hurting herself and others, but I still could not be sure of her motives. I knew Johannes and Amelia had begun to spend a little time together, and I had hoped she could learn to appreciate him. But now I had second thoughts about Johannes and Amelia, for I was afraid she could no longer be trusted. She seemed to twist things in her mind, and instead of being grateful for the opportunity I had given her here, she only seemed to want more. I had wanted Amelia as a protégée, but had I only succeeded in kindling her ambitions? Perhaps I had been blind. Perhaps she wanted to run the hotel herself just as she wanted David for herself. If such were the case, she would have a very strong motive for wanting me out of her way.

CHAPTER SEVENTEEN

IN THE AFTERNOON, I went out to the back porch where I unexpectedly found David watching Pepys operate the mowing machine.

"Oh," I said, "you startled me!"

"I am sorry. You didn't say good-night last night, Erika. Are you all right?"

"Yes, I was tired and went to bed early. That is all."

He frowned. "I must go to Mulgrove House and read your mother's diary."

I blushed, looking down. "Yes, I think you should see it." Then I raised my face to his. "I spoke to my father. He had returned from a voyage at the time I was conceived." I could not look David in the eye, but he turned my head back to face him.

"Then he confirms that we are not blood related?"

"He would never *confirm* it, but it seems we are not."

"I am relieved. Erika," he said. He slipped his hand around my waist and pulled me closer, his gaze traveling from my eyes down to my lips. I found myself leaning against him as our passion quickened. But we had to hold back, for we were in plain view of the hotel.

"When will you go?" I asked.

He loosened his hold on me. "As soon as possible. I must carry out some investigations of my own—having to do with my own father."

"Oh, of course." I hadn't thought of it, but now that we knew Gerhard Langermann had been faithful to his wife, there was the rest of the puzzle to solve. If he had been faithful to his wife, why had he met Julie Ann at the windmill the night she died?

He took my hands and lifted my fingers to his lips, and the look he gave me was so full of emotion that I felt my heart contract.

"Perhaps soon we will be able to put the past truly behind us," he said.

"Do you think it's possible?"

"Surely you must know by now that I want to marry you, Erika."

My heart leaped as bittersweet tears glistened in my eyes. I could hardly speak as he pressed me against him. "Oh, David, it is what I wanted, but I did not believe it could ever be so."

He gave me a wry smile. "Even so, your father would not approve, would he?"

"No." My jaw tightened. I feared my father's reaction to such news. He seemed to hate David and everything he stood for.

"It does not take much to perceive the bad feeling that exists between us," David said. "Whatever was between your family and mine still exists. It is that which I seek to resolve before we can be truly happy."

"You are right, of course." I closed my eyes, the sun warming my face as we stood contentedly for a few minutes more. Just before we went in, I turned to glance over my shoulder to see that Pepys was still watching us.

The sky clouded over in the late afternoon. I shut my windows and watched the oncoming storm while I dressed for dinner.

Then I moved to the stairs. Just as I was about to descend, I caught my heel on something and stumbled. I cried out as I fell, and two of the guests who were coming up the stairs watched in horror as my feet flew out from under me and I twisted in an effort to clutch at the banister.

The gentleman rushed forward to catch me, but not before I hit my head on the railing as I sat down awkwardly.

"Are you all right, miss?" he asked as I caught my breath.

"I think so." I touched my head, feeling more embarrassment than pain. He assisted me to my feet.

"Ah, look, here is the culprit." He picked up a piece of metal pipe and held it at arm's length. I frowned.

"How stupid of someone to leave this on the stair. Give it to me."

I refused his offer to escort me to my room, took the pipe and sent for Letty to bring me some ice for my head. Then I sat and stared at the object, wondering how it had come to be on the stair.

After seeing that the bump on my head was not serious, I descended to the dining room, more carefully this time. By the time dinner was over and the dining room closed for the evening, I was exhausted. Every muscle ached as I pulled my weight upstairs. Once in my cambric dressing gown, I let my hair down and brushed it out gingerly. The bump on the side of my head was tender, but the ice had helped.

I heard the rat-a-tat of rain on the windowpanes, and I moved to the window. A thick mist was still blowing in from the east, and the moon's light, diffracted by the fog, spread a ghostly light from behind the clouds. I gazed through the glass at the blackness, shivering slightly. The night affected me strangely, but I shook off the feeling and went to bed. After all, hadn't David just told me he wanted to marry me? The thought should bring me joy, and yet with so much unsettled, it did not.

ON THE FRIDAY NIGHT FOLLOWING I wore my new yellow silk gauze gown with yellow satin roses holding up the train. The dress gave me confidence as I chatted with guests from New York. It was late when I finally went to my room, and not feeling sleepy, I changed into my dressing gown, opened my windows wide and reclined on my daybed with a book. I was deep into the story when I heard it. Tinkling music that floated down to me through my open window. There was no party in the ballroom tonight, no musicians playing.

I listened to the familiar notes for some seconds before I rose and walked to the window. Standing there, I had a better idea of which direction the sound came from. Then quickly I crossed my room, opened the door to the hallway and moved toward the stairs. I could hear the faint notes drifting down to me as I climbed, the sound filling me with determination to discover its source this time.

No longer was I afraid of it. I did not believe there was anything supernatural about it. The music, ghostly as it might sound, came from a human source—a source I was determined to discover.

I reached the ballroom and flung open the doors. "Who's there?" I called, my voice echoing in the darkness. I strode onto the polished wood floor and moved toward the stage, its gold curtains drawn back to reveal empty music stands.

The music stopped. As before, the far set of French doors had been left open. A ghost does not need to open doors, I reasoned. My heart pounding, I moved toward the open doors.

"I will not be frightened off this time," I said out loud. The balcony was empty, but as I stepped out, I heard a noise to my left as if something had come loose and fallen off the roof. I looked up.

"Is someone there?"

I saw nothing, but I moved along the balcony to the place I thought I had heard the sound. Several bricks jutted like stairs to the roof above the concrete railing.

It would be more sensible to wait until daylight and to send one of the men up there, but if I waited, my quarry would be gone, and if there was a hiding place accessible from the roof, I might not be able to find it. I had to follow now, assuming there actually was someone ahead of me, someone who had kicked loose a piece of shingle from the roof.

My heart beat rapidly. My determination to find out what was going on and who was doing it overcame caution. I had always been surefooted, and my anger drove me forward. I grasped the handholds and hoisted myself onto the railing. I knew enough not to look down, and instead I focused on the stairlike bricks, testing each one carefully before putting my weight on it.

I clambered onto the roof and lay full-length over the shingles, using my foot to shove myself along. The shingles tore at my dressing gown, but I made it to safety. I lay still for a minute, catching my breath, then looked about me. The kitchen roofs were below to my right. I told myself that should I slip there was less of a drop to the kitchen roofs than to the ground.

As I looked above me the blood plumped through my veins. I knew I was doing a dangerous thing, but I could not go back now. I was sure someone had come this way before me, and my anger and frustration drove me to look for traces of the way the person might have gone.

I crawled along the roof to the nearest gable, then crouched in the corner formed where the gable jutted from the roof. I wondered if my quarry had disappeared through the window of the gable into the attic, but there were only a few inches of shingle between the gable window and the drop-off to the balcony below. I could not see how anyone could have gone that way, and I was not going to risk it.

My eyes had grown used to the darkness now, and I examined the outline of the roof, following it with my eyes to the west chimney. Then I remembered that there were two gables like this one on the other side, and a door in the roof between them, leading to the attic.

I summoned my courage and crawled up the roof. I reached the top and pulled myself gradually until I could lift my legs over to the other side. Then I again lay along the shingles, catching my breath. It had started to rain slightly, making the roof more slippery. The gables were off to my right, and they seemed farther than the one that had sheltered me on the other side. The wind was coming up as well, and I had to move very carefully. I did not relish tumbling onto the roof of the porch below, perhaps to be tossed to my death on the circular gravel drive in front of the hotel. As it was, I knew I must be mad to be up here alone, but I could not stop to think about it.

My feet slid more than once so that I had to grab the roof edge and hang on desperately until I regained my balance. Then in one mad scramble, I made the first gable and hung on to its arch, crouching in the corner.

I was shaking now as I realized the desperation of my attempt.

When my mind cleared a little and I looked about me, I could see the door in the side of the roof. I had seen Johannes's workmen walking upright on this slope, but in work boots and in the light of day. I was not about to try to stand up. I let myself slide down the roof slowly, afraid that any moment I would pitch to my death, but finally my feet rested on the upper frame of the door, and I rested my head in my arms, sobbing in relief.

After my hysteria had subsided somewhat, I made sure my footing was secure and then scooted down beside the door. I was afraid it might be latched from the inside, but it wasn't, and the hinge squealed as I pulled the door open to let it fall back on the roof with a thud. Then I sat on the lower edge, my feet dangling through the dark opening. Trembling, I sought and found the ladder below me. There was no light, and while outside I had the faint moonlight to help me, inside the attic it was pitch-black.

But now that I had come this far I could not go down any other way than by the attic itself. I knew it was foolish to step into a dark room where someone might be waiting for me. How easy for them to clasp their hand over my mouth and their fingers about my throat. How easy to snuff out my life just as my mother's had been. I shuddered.

A sudden movement above startled me, and I smothered a scream. The figure of a man was silhouetted on the edge of the roof. Then he lowered himself to make his way down the slope.

Panic seized me. Without thinking, I descended into the darkness of the attic. I crouched at the bottom of the ladder, every muscle tense. Nothing moved in the room where I hovered.

CHAPTER EIGHTEEN

"ERIKA," A MAN'S VOICE called. "Are you all right?"

I looked at the opening above me where a figure crouched. My heart beat in my chest at an alarming rate.

"Erika, it's Johannes." As he lowered his feet to the top step of the ladder, I began to shriek, but I clapped my hand over my mouth. Johannes. Still, I stepped back instinctively as he descended the ladder.

"Johannes," I finally said.

"I saw you go out on the balcony. When I saw you take to the roof, I followed as fast as I could, but you had a head start on me."

"You gave me a scare," I said in a voice that still shook.

"I have a match." I heard him strike it and then a small flame blazed in front of me. His eyes darted around as he held the flame to illuminate the garret we were in.

"It's an attic room," I said somewhat stupidly, thinking that since I was unharmed I should at least enlist Johannes's help.

When the match burned out, he lit another. There was no furniture in the room except a broken chair and some old sacking material. But my eye caught sight of something on the floor in the corner.

"Look," I said, pointing to it. Then our light went out. Johannes struck another match and I reached for the kerosene lamp that stood ready for use. I held it while he lit the wick, then I adjusted it until the light grew steady.

"Why did you climb up here?" asked Johannes.

"I heard the music that sometimes plays in the ballroom, and I followed it. There wasn't anyone in the ballroom, but the balcony doors were open. Then I thought I heard someone scrambling on the roof and it looked to me like someone had climbed up that way."

"Why didn't you call for help?" he asked.

"I thought I could surprise whoever it was. No one would expect me to follow them up to the roof, and I was angry." I sighed. "I know it was foolish, but I wanted to know who plays that awful music and how they do it."

Johannes frowned, but refrained from passing judgment on my reckless act. Instead he examined the room we were in, with its pitched roof, then he ducked through a low doorway that led to the rest of the attic. I followed.

We both had to crouch a little to avoid hitting our heads on the thick supporting beams. When we held the light over the floor I could see that other footsteps had come this way, for there were prints in the thick layer of dust.

"Look," I said, pointing them out.

He nodded. "But there's no one here now. Whoever climbed over the roof had enough time to come this way before you could catch up to them."

"Yes, I suppose." I shivered. "There is someone, then, isn't there? I mean the music. It's not a ghost."

He shrugged. "I'll have a look after I've seen you safely to your room."

"No, Johannes. I'll not stand by helplessly while you hunt for my assailant. I'll search with you. Besides, I am familiar with this part of the hotel, if memory serves me."

He frowned at the dark corners around us. "Very well, but stay behind me."

I held the lantern so we could search every corner of the attic. But there was no other signs. We took the ladder to the floor below and inspected the corridor where we stood next to the ballroom. I noticed a side door I had forgotten about earlier.

"Look," I said to Johannes. "This leads to the stage."

I pushed it open, and the lamp illumined a small stairwell to the stage. A narrow passage led behind the stage, and I held the lamp before me, hesitant to set foot there even though it had been cleaned out during the renovations.

Holding the lamp higher, I saw an object lying on the floor to our left. It was a large wooden box with carving on the side. My heart beat rapidly as we walked toward it.

Johannes knelt and fingered the latch on the box. Even before he lifted the lid I knew what I would hear, for hadn't I seen a similar, although smaller, box at Mulgrove House?

The lid came back to reveal a broken statue of a ballerina, turning to the music that poured forth. I stared in fascination as the waltz that had haunted me played. A chill ran down my spine, for even though I knew now that no ghostly specter was making the music, I knew something worse. Whoever played it was someone in the hotel.

"I've heard enough," I said.

He shut the lid, and the music stopped. "You say you've heard this music from your room?"

I nodded. "It's not loud enough to carry from this spot, but if someone took it out to the balcony..." I looked at Johannes. "Evidently whoever it was came back here first to hide the music box, then went through the French doors to the roof."

He looked at me curiously, and I knew he thought I might be mistaken. But I shook my head. "No, Johannes, I'm sure there was someone. The person passed through the French doors onto the balcony just ahead of me."

"Then whoever it was must have meant to lure you onto the roof, to put you in danger of falling off."

"Yes," I said, realizing how nearly the culprit had succeeded.

"I'll take the box downstairs for you. Then I'm going to have another look up here."

"I'd like to show it to Maude," I said, studying the menacing thing.

I held the light so he could carry the music box out. It had started to rain in earnest now, but we went along to Maude and Teddy's quarters and I tapped lightly on the door. To my surprise, when Maude came to open the door, in her dressing gown and nightcap, I saw David standing in the light cast by the globe lamp on the table in the center of the room.

Maude pushed her spectacles up on her nose when she saw me, and then she peered behind me at Johannes.

"David," I said.

"It was so late," he said, coming to me, "that I didn't want to disturb you when I arrived. I saw the light on in the cottage, so I came to see if Mr. and Mrs. Jordan were still up."

"Johannes and I have found something I thought Maude should see."

Johannes placed the music box on the table, and Teddy shuffled over in his slippers. I raised the lid. The waltz played, and Maude stared at it, her face pale, and then she looked at me.

I shut the lid. "Yes. This is our ghostly music."

"But how could it be?"

"Very simple. Someone hid the music box behind the stage or perhaps in one of the rooms when the workmen were there, and when they wished to play it, they set it on the balcony, so the sound would carry to the rooms below. You would even be able to hear it in this cottage on a clear night."

She was trembling, and I hated to upset her, but I wanted her to see for herself how it had been done.

"Who?" she asked.

"It had to be someone who was at the hotel before I came here." Maude had said she'd heard the music in the weeks before I arrived. I realized now that if that were the case then Amelia, at least, had not been responsible for the music.

She looked at me, her eyes filled with pity. "Pepys was the only one here."

"Johannes," I said, "please go to the stables and see if Pepys is there now. Ask if he's had anything to do with this."

"You can bring him here," said Teddy, standing straighter.

Johannes went to the stables and Maude moved to poke the fire in the stone fireplace and put on some tea. The wind was howling now, and in a few moments there was a rattle and the door opened. But it wasn't Johannes who entered. It was my father. He stood blinking his eyes in the light. No one moved.

"Father," I said, "what are you doing here?"

"Seen the lights on."

"Please come in. David is here, too."

David cleared his throat. "I'm glad you're here, Captain Barlow. I wanted to speak to you . . . about the misunderstanding you've allowed to persist about your daughter's birth."

My father jutted his chin forward. "I wouldn't know what misunderstanding you're talking about. When she was born, I claimed her as my own. What else could I do?"

"But you knew that rumors persisted to the contrary."

"My wife earned her own reputation."

"That may be, but you also had Erika to think of."

"I knew she'd be cursed with her mother's blood. Even so I left her all my property to do with as she pleased when she was old enough."

"And it never would have been yours at all if Erika's grandfather hadn't bought the land, built the hotel and handed it to you," David said, the muscles in his face tightening.

My father moved toward the table, his eyes flitting about the room.

"Now that we know Erika's true parentage," David continued, "that she and I are not half brother and sister as we once thought, we plan to marry."

My father began to tremble and bluster, his eyes blinking madly. "You're stubborn, like your mother was," he growled at me. "Devil take you."

"I'm sorry that my mother did not bring you happiness," I said. "But surely that is no reason to deny me mine."

"Is there not something else you wish to tell us, Captain?" David demanded.

I looked up questioningly at David. My father stared straight ahead, looking at nothing as a long hoarse rattle escaped him.

David strode to him and gripped one of his arms. "If you wish your daughter to find any happiness, you must say what you have to say. The fear of incest has finally been removed from our hearts, but that is not enough. There is another shadow we will live under the rest of our lives unless you are prepared to speak the truth."

My father was trembling violently now. Then he spoke just loud enough so that we could hear him. "I killed her," he said. "If that's what you want to know."

"What?" I moved forward, not certain I had heard him correctly, but he looked at his hands, which he had turned palms up in front of him.

"I choked the breath from her so that she could sin no more. I let her lover come to her to gaze on her body one last time, only she could no longer respond to his sinful caress. I can say it now, for what have I to lose? I did the deed."

I froze in horror. I must have stared at him for a full minute as my heart thundered in my chest and the blood threatened to burst my eardrums. Time seemed to stop as my father's eyes met mine, and then I saw everything clearly for the first time. I saw that he was mad. Finally, I whispered through dry lips, "You."

"She deserved it, you know. Unfaithful, she was, and she passed on her evil to you."

"No," I said, my hands reaching out in front of me. "No," I cried louder. But David held my arms as I unleashed the torment of words and emotion. "She loved Gerhard Langermann, it's true, but he couldn't come to her after he married. If you'd been kind and patient," I sobbed, "you could have won her love, you could have!"

I was sobbing hysterically and I threw off David's hands. "You beat her and you drank!" I yelled. "Could you not have tried to understand her? She could have loved you...."

Great sobs escaped me as the room spun. Then I found myself in David's arms again. The terrible truth struck me. My father had somehow tricked Julie Ann and Gerhard. He had lured them to the windmill, and instead of their consoling each other over their lost happiness, Gerhard had found her dead.

My father was circling the room, wringing his hands. "He still wanted the shameless wench. His willpower to stay away from her was weakened by the dull life he had. She still wrote him letters, she did, and I slipped in a page. Then I forged a note from him and I watched her as she read it. How I hated her when her face colored and she ran to her rendezvous. I knew what I had to do."

He stopped pacing and faced us as I clung to David's arm, feeling sick at the thought that my own father was a murderer. Then I realized the worst. He had tried to kill me, too, put an end to my passion as he had Julie Ann's.

"I killed her," he muttered. "Left her there for that man to find her. You were my daughter, but you had her evil in you. She was dead, but I had to do it all over again. I knew you'd come back. It wasn't hard to lose myself along the docks of New York after I found my way back from the Aucklands. I knew you'd come and I knew what I'd have to do.''

The room swayed, and I walked unsteadily across it. But he only gave me a dazed look.

"You played the music, too, didn't you, father?"

"Music?" He moved toward me, and though my heart was hammering, I stood my ground.

"You wanted to frighten me, didn't you?" I went on. "You must have lied about when you came here. You were here already, hiding, waiting for me. You tried to kill me that night by the boat house. You must have stalked me the night of Major Ward's party. And you started the fire that could have killed me and destroyed the hotel." I paused for a moment, remembering guiltily that I had thought Amelia behind this last. Then I uttered, "Why, Father?"

He came forward, his hands outstretched. "You've guessed the truth. I made my way here at night. Weird it was to see this place after all those years. Still it all came back. I climbed the outside stairs to the roof. Got into the attic. I had plenty of time to go over the place, and no one knew I was here. Then I found this." He pushed passed me and reached for the music box. Before we could stop him, he picked it up and clutched it to his chest.

"Her father gave the other one to her," he muttered, looking dazedly at us, but seeing no one. "She said she lost it so he'd get her another, but she gave it to her lover."

Suddenly he turned and bolted for the door.

"Father, wait!" I shrieked.

But he had stumbled out of the cottage into the rain. The storm was upon us now, and when the lightning flashed, I could see him heading for the wharf.

"Father," I called, "come back!" David and I started down the path, squinting through the driving rain as thunder cracked around us. By the time we reached the wharf, my father had already untied the only rowboat.

As we ran along the wharf trying to catch him, he climbed into the boat and pushed off. He had set the music box on the seat with him. The lid had come open, and as we reached the end of the wharf, the tinkling music floated eerily up from the waves.

"Father!" I half sobbed as I heard the splash of oars and he pulled himself into the now-blinding storm.

"We've got to do something," I shouted to David.

"Where are the other boats?" he shouted back.

"In the boat house."

Johannes joined us on the wharf, and he and David started for the boat house. I stood shivering on the end of the dock, fearful now that the storm would take them all.

Suddenly there was a jagged bolt of lightning and a dreadful crash of thunder. In a paralyzing moment of horror I saw the lightning strike my father, who was standing in the rowboat, his arms upraised as if cursing the heavens above. I screamed as I saw him fall toward the water. Then there was a second flash of lightning. It illumined the rowboat, now empty but for the music box that still sat on the seat. My father was nowhere in sight. I knew he was dead.

David and Johannes, too, had witnessed the horrible event. They now pulled their boat to the wharf, and David climbed out beside me.

"It's too late!" David shouted in my ear. "There's nothing we can do. No one could have survived that."

I was sobbing and choking, and the water was splashing at our feet as we stumbled back toward the path. We made the lighted cottage and Maude and Teddy led me to a chair.

"He's gone," I said.

"Lord 'a mercy," Maude said, who had seen everything from her window.

"Perhaps it is better this way," said Teddy gently, placing a hand on Maude's arm.

She nodded wordlessly, then he said, "Miss Erika should be getting out of her wet clothes." He half turned Maude and drew her in my direction, and then she nodded and crossed to put her arm about me.

She led me to her and Teddy's bedroom, and I moved like a zombie, incapable even of saying good-night to the others. Maude helped me change into something of hers, then put me to bed then and there, holding my hand while I lay back and closed my eyes. I didn't think I would sleep that night, but the pictures that swam in my mind became dreams, and then sometime in the early hours of the morning, I dozed, with Maude sleeping in the chair next to me.

When I awoke, the sun was forcing its way into the room around the edge of the curtains, and I heard the murmur of voices in the front room. I closed my eyes, turning my head into the pillow, trying to shut out the voices, but without success.

I heard Maude and Teddy, but the other voice was deeper, speaking in decisive tones. My eyelids fluttered open, and I reached to pull the covers back as the door swung wide and David came in. He closed the distance between us and caught my hand before I could pull the sheet up around me.

I felt the tears threaten to engulf me as he pulled me to him. "I didn't want it to be true that my father was a murderer," I spluttered, "that he killed my mother, that he tried to kill me, but it is true, isn't it? I have to learn to face that fact."

"I'm sorry, Erika. I wish it could be otherwise. But I thought you would want to know the truth. I learned that your father left the *Merry Weather* a year before he told us he did."

"I just need a little time to understand what's happened."

"I love you, my darling," he said. "But I will not rush you. I can see that rushing headlong into a love affair cannot be right. We must walk steadily toward each other, having learned the lesson of recklessness and what it cost our parents."

I smiled through my tears, warmed by his love and the tenderness of his embrace. "And yet you must admit we have inherited some of their passions," I said, raising my head to look into his eyes.

He allowed himself a small smile, but said, "Passions we will hold in check until the time is right."

I swallowed, still dizzy from all that had happened, but already feeling my heart beat in anticipation of David's loving caresses. But I, too, held on to my feelings, wanting time to order my thoughts, to plan for the future.

"Oh, David," I said and lifted my arms to encircle his neck as I laid my cheek against his. We sat thus for a moment, and then I raised my head and slipped out of his arms.

"How did you know?" I asked. "You forced my father's admission out of him. Why didn't you speak before?"

He released my hands and stood, looking down at me. "For years I turned my back on the murder, ignored the rumors. But then you came into my life," he said. "When I met you I knew I could turn my back no longer. You made me face those events. Of course I had always thought it odd that my father did not try to defend himself in any way at the trial. He could have said she drove him to it, that they had argued. But he said nothing. They assumed he had lost his mind, and perhaps he did lose it the night he found her dead like that. Perhaps he even believed he killed her. I began to wonder if there was more to the matter, so I decided to investigate it."

"But how?"

"My father's lawyer. He still practices in New York. He was glad to tell me what he knew. He had never got my father to say more than that he didn't know if he killed Julie Ann. Apparently after he arrived at the windmill, all he remembered was kneeling by her body, not how she came to die. That's how they found him of course, just kneeling there, staring at her, his hands touching her throat. And they thought he had killed her."

"How awful."

"Yes. He might have killed her, but he didn't know. Then the lawyer remembered the letters."

"Letters?"

"My father wrote them to me from prison. They were intercepted by the prison keeper and only sent to my mother two years after my father was hanged. She read them and then gave them to my father's lawyer to keep.''

"Why didn't she show them to you?''

He shrugged, his face a mask of irony. "Who can say? Perhaps she didn't think I should read them after all that time, for fear it would open old wounds. For nothing would bring him back then. And perhaps most of all, she herself wanted to forget.''

"What did the letters say?''

I saw the pain flash across David's eyes as he thought of his father, but he seemed determined to continue. "They were strange, halting letters, as if he were very unsure of himself by then. But he said he loved me and he was sorry for the misfortune he had brought on his family, and he hoped that someday I would forgive him. He said he did not think he could have killed Julie Ann, that he believed it to be some trick of Fate.''

"I see.''

"The letters themselves would have proved nothing if the real murderer had not confessed.''

I shook my head and looked at him helplessly. He sat on the bed next to me and reached out to take my chin in his hand.

"They're searching for your father's body now.''

We were silent for a few moments, during which I sent out my own private prayer for my father's spirit, which I knew would wander painfully, looking for peace.

"I'm not sorry it had to happen this way,'' David said, "if it means you're out of danger.''

We sat for a few more moments, our hands clasped, contemplating the awful turn of events. Then he brought his lips to mine gently and kissed me tenderly. How I wanted to hold him next to me all day, seeking the comfort that only lovers can give each other, but I knew that now we should wait until our marriage had sanctioned our love for each other. And so I released him, raising my face to kiss his beloved lips once more.

There was a knock on the door. I reached for the robe at my feet and called, "Come in."

David bade me goodbye. "I have business in Greenport, but I will return this evening. I hope you will dine with me."

I nodded, clutching the robe to my chest.

Maude laid a bundle of clothing on my bed. "Letty brought these for you to put on." She unfolded a fresh blue and white linen day dress along with fresh lingerie.

"Thank you, Maude."

She helped me into the clothes, fastening the many hooks and eyes, and then I brushed my hair and coiled it on the back of my head. I felt a dull weight in my chest, but I knew that the best thing to do would be to get back to work. I knew I must make things at the hotel appear as normal as possible. When I finished dressing and went out the front of the cottage, Amelia was waiting for me.

"I came here early this morning to see about you," she said, "but Maude told me you needed your rest."

I smiled at her.

"Oh, Erika," she said, coming to take my hands, "I'm so sorry to hear what's happened. Are you all right?"

"I'm fine, Amelia, and I'm glad to see you." She grasped my hands tightly and we looked at each other. I knew that the emotion I saw in her face was honest.

She moistened her lips. "I didn't realize the danger you were in. It truly frightened me to hear it. Erika, I've been terribly foolish. I was jealous of you, but for no good reason.''

Tears stung my eyes. ''You had no reason to be jealous.''

''I realize that now. I'm afraid I rather lost my head. It was filled with fantasies I had no right to have.''

I squeezed her hands. ''I'm glad you've told me. I'm sure we can put things right.''

She lifted her head, meeting my gaze tentatively. ''I hope you still consider me worthy of your friendship.''

''Of course I do. I've always wanted you to be my friend.''

She smiled warmly at me and then we hugged each other. I could hardly contain my happiness at restoring the friendship I had so hoped for, but had thought was lost.

CHAPTER NINETEEN

DAVID AND I STOOD on the deck of the steamer as she pulled out of New York harbor. The city seemed very large and crowded to me after the insular feeling I had grown used to on the North Fork. But I had enjoyed spending the second night of our honeymoon in one of New York's finest elegant hotels where we could move about in complete anonymity as lovers like to do.

I leaned back and David tucked his arm around my waist, holding me against him possessively. "What are you thinking, my darling?" he asked as the crowded skyline gradually became smaller.

"I am thinking I am already enjoying being Mrs. David Langermann." We had been married quietly at Mulgrove House with Amelia, Johannes, Maude and Teddy in attendance. Amelia pleaded that she and Johannes, whom I had named as managers of the hotel in my absence, would not be able to do half the job I could, but I assured them that I had faith in their abilities.

Maude had wept a torrent, insisting they were tears of happiness as they all saw us off in the carriage bound for New York. David had turned his affairs over to a capable manager, and we were leaving for London for an extended stay. But I promised Maude and the others that we would return in time to open the hotel next summer.

"You must lead the grand ball," she told me with tears in her eyes.

"Of course we will," I said, looking into her eyes. I knew what she was thinking. No longer would Julie Ann's spirit need to trouble any of us. For with the truth revealed at last, her spirit had found peace.

Tears moistened my eyes as I pressed closer to David. He nuzzled my cheek with his chin. It was time to create our own future together.

ATTRACTIVE, SPACE SAVING BOOK RACK

Display your most prized novels on this handsome and sturdy book rack. The hand-rubbed walnut finish will blend into your library decor with quiet elegance, providing a practical organizer for your favorite hard-or soft-covered books.

Only $9.95

Approximately 16" x 8" when assembled.

Assembles in seconds!

To order, rush your name, address and zip code, along with a check or money order for $10.70* ($9.95 plus 75¢ postage and handling) payable to *Harlequin Reader Service*:

Harlequin Reader Service
Book Rack Offer
901 Fuhrmann Blvd.
P.O. Box 1396
Buffalo, NY 14269-1396

Offer not available in Canada.

*New York and Iowa residents add appropriate sales tax.

PAMELA BROWNING

...is fireworks on the green at the Fourth of July and prayers said around the Thanksgiving table. It is the dream of freedom realized in thousands of small towns across this great nation.

But mostly, the Heartland is its people. People who care about and help one another. People who cherish traditional values and give to their children the greatest gift, the gift of love.

American Romance presents HEARTLAND, an emotional trilogy about people whose memories, hopes and dreams are bound up in the acres they farm.

HEARTLAND...the story of America.

Don't miss these heartfelt stories: American Romance #237 SIMPLE GIFTS (March), #241 FLY AWAY (April), and #245 HARVEST HOME (May).

Penny Jordan

Stronger than Yearning

He was the man of her dreams!

The same dark hair, the same mocking eyes; it was as if the Regency rake of the portrait, the seducer of Jenna's dream, had come to life. Jenna, believing the last of the Deverils dead, was determined to buy the great old Yorkshire Hall—to claim it for her daughter, Lucy, and put to rest some of the painful memories of Lucy's birth. She had no way of knowing that a direct descendant of the black sheep Deveril even existed—or that James Allingham and his own powerful yearnings would disrupt her plan entirely.

Penny Jordan's first Harlequin Signature Edition *Love's Choices* was an outstanding success. Penny Jordan has written more than 40 best-selling titles—more than 4 million copies sold.

Now, be sure to buy her latest bestseller, *Stronger Than Yearning*. Available wherever paperbacks are sold—in June.

COMING SOON

Harlequin Historicals

Exciting, adventurous, sensual stories of love long ago.

Be sure to look for them this July wherever you buy Harlequin Books—you won't want to miss out.